I Died Yesterday

Pamela Norton Docken

Pamela Norton Docken

This novel is dedicated to my loved ones who have passed before me. You are my light.

Pamela Norton Docken

Pamela Norton Docken

Prologue

We are all of one soul, but with many avenues in which our souls travel. Life is never-ending; just a reshaping of the way we perceive it. We look up to the heavens because that is where we are truly at home, our time on earth yet another journey in a series of many – to learn to live, love, forgive, and move forward to bettering ourselves and our collective soul.

Our petty worries are just that: petty. We all have the capability to change who we are *no matter who we are*. From those who passed before us to those who pass with us and for those yet to come, we follow the river of life with every twist and turn, every rapid raging bend, and sometimes calm waters. We often take in the ugly while never looking for the beauty and the blessing of life. As the rivers flow into the oceans, our souls flow into the afterlife, the end of this life as we know it to become one with the larger body and continue to live on in another place and time. You might ask how I would know this and I wouldn't blame you. The answer is simple: I died yesterday.

YESTERDAY

Chapter One

You heard me right. I died yesterday. Croaked, passed away, departed; whatever you want to call it. The fact is, I stopped breathing, my heart stopped beating, and I ceased living. The process wasn't at all what I expected; not at all.

Moments seemed like hours and hours like minutes. All the questions I ever had, everything I ever struggled with in life, every "why," "what," or "how come" I ever had would be answered in ways I would have never imagined.

The most astounding thing is that I have just a moment, one speck in time, to share my experience with you before it is all gone and wiped from my memory. I don't know why I am allowed to tell you what to look for in your journey through this thing we call life, as it is beyond my understanding.

However, I do know it's something any human with a soul has wondered about from the beginning of time. By the grace of God, I get to share what lies ahead. *The question is, will you hear me?*

You may wonder how, if I died, am I able to write this for the entire world to see. It's possible because the powers that be bring us together in the beauty of a thing we call life.

It's not a miracle; it just is. An open soul is like an open door. I have found the perfect human to document my journey. I encourage you to open your mind and heart to hear what I am about to say.

I must speak quickly as I only have a short amount of time to share this with you, since it's already beginning to fade in my memory.

Chapter Two

So you may better understand my journey, I want to tell you a little about my former life when I was still breathing. I was not much different from half the population. You could say I was a working-class girl who would never break the glass ceiling. I lived paycheck to paycheck and lived in a tiny one-bedroom apartment above an old hardware store with wooden stairs that moaned and creaked every time I walked up or down them. I lived alone, never meeting that one true love. I doubted there even was such a thing.

My life was routine, hardly ever deviated, and if it did, it was by chance, not by choice. Every morning: get up, go to work, come home, eat, stare at the meaningless television, go to bed, repeat daily.

I had nothing going for me, or at least that was what I thought as I ungratefully walked through what was my life. I did not realize what an angry, negative human I had been.

The world was black and white to me, the cup never half full. I was incapable of seeing the beauty of the sunrise, hearing the music of the wind, or even enjoying the babble of a creek.

My only belief in God was there was no God, because how and why would a loving God put me through all the pain and misery known as my life?

I now realize I had forgotten my core, my soul, and the power of God was within me all along, as it is with everyone. How is it that it's so easy never to acknowledge your soul, the very core of your being, the thing that makes you unique, that makes all of us unique?

Why is it so simple to ignore all that is within us and live our lives based on material things, man-made ideals and rules, which, in actuality, don't apply to anything, yet choose to be blind by not acknowledging the beauty of our souls?

It is our souls that give us the profound ability to see the real possibility of heaven on earth, *if only we choose to see it, live it.* For some reason, we choose not to see; we close our eyes tightly and shutter our hearts to the wonder of what we are, only to make us who we are – a world of lost souls.

The refusal to see, to acknowledge our self, is the reason for wars, anger, fear, hate, starvation, and prejudice.

I say "we" because this is about all of us, not just me – for every one of us who has forgotten what our soul truly is and from where it came. I now realize I had it all wrong from the beginning of my life until the very end.

My life, my time on earth could be viewed as a waste of something so precious, a gift that had been made just for me. But it was much more than that, and this is why I am here to tell you my story.

What I now see is a clean slate and, for me to begin writing on it, I must finish who I am so I can be who I will be. So I can move on.

In this life – now I guess you could say "my past life" – I truly was an angry woman. Bitterness was my closest and dearest friend.

I belittled myself time and again at my lack of education, my disgust in my appearance, the shame and disdain I had for my family. There was also the disappointment of not knowing love and intolerance of those not like me, not understanding me – all which I had allowed to consume me.

And what did I think of the world around me? It didn't exist. I never cared at all about what plight was happening in the world; who shot who in the daily murders that never failed to occur each and every moment somewhere across the world, even the one that happened in my neighborhood.

I didn't care who was starving now or who was begging for money or food; no, none of those things mattered to me. The only thing that did matter was the fact that I was not happy with the life bestowed upon me.

Those feelings, those thoughts, the overpowering anger that so consumed my soul is now long gone, now nothing but a vague memory, and for that, I am elated.

I finally know my purpose, and that is to let you know what awaits you. Soon enough, I will once again become a fresh slate with a new beginning given to me and I hope you will have that opportunity when it's your time to move on.

I have found our collective soul forgives the ignorance of our past and sends each of us on to another experience to learn, to grow, to be one with our soul.

For the first time in my existence, what some would call faith, is a part of me. Telling you my story and sharing the experience of my death with you may just make your journey through this life a better one.

I will share with you everything I went through and how it allowed me to unburden myself so that I could move on. To be honest, I don't know at this moment where I will go from here, but I am so close to finding out, I can hardly contain myself.

For now, for this moment in time, all I know is for sure is the old me is no longer with you, and the new me is just beginning. Soon, outside of love, I will not remember my past at all, and that is just fine. I embrace the fact that though I may not remember, the life I am leaving has prepared me for my journey forward.

Chapter Three

My day started out like any other. I must admit, I am not a morning person – never have been – so it doesn't take much to throw me off for the day. And so it was on my last day on earth.

My old digital clock with the numbers that flip every minute with a quiet little click sat on my nightstand like a fox, just biding its time, waiting for the right time to blast its alarm and startle me awake.

It seemed to come so suddenly when, at 6:30 am, like a siren, the damned thing screeched on and on. Not wanting to wake, I tried in vain to silence it. Blindly, I reached about my nightstand in the dark in an attempt to hit to snooze button to end the ever-annoying sound coming from it.

I should have turned on a light to see what I was doing, but in my groggy state, I didn't think it necessary. I reasoned that though the bedroom was dark, it wasn't nighttime dark, more like a gray dawn seeping through my window blinds, seemingly just enough light for me to be able to see what I was doing.

The fact is, there wasn't enough light to clearly see anything. I am as blind as a bat without my glasses, and that was my downfall.

In my attempt to silence the beastly alarm, I failed to notice the bottle of water sitting precariously on the edge of my nightstand, a silent sentinel waiting for a catastrophe to happen.

I blindly reached out and knocked the bottle over with my hand, effectively soaking everything on the nightstand. As the water spread across the nightstand, I put my hand squarely into a huge pile of used Kleenex, now drenched by the bottle's water. I should have tossed them out a week ago. I cursed myself for not throwing away the remnants of last week's head cold.

Worst of all, my clumsiness caused the water to pool around my precious iPod, surely seeping into whatever crack or crevice it would find.

I sat up in disbelief, repeatedly demeaning myself in my head for what I had done, and outwardly scolding myself for not turning on the light first instead of just blindly reaching out in my futile attempt to silence that annoying sound.

If only I had known then that, within the next hour, I wasn't going to ever need that gadget or my precious glasses again, it might not have mattered so much to me.

But I didn't know dying was on the agenda for the day, so I was angry over my never-ending clumsiness. After further inspection, I noticed two pictures of my vacation that had lain on the table were also wet.

In frustration, I picked up those pictures and cursed again. I made a futile attempt to make up for my sloppiness by grabbing a handful of soggy candy wrappers that had been strewn about the table from my middle-of-the-night eating binges and threw them in the direction of the little trashcan I kept in my room. I missed it by a mile, leaving the candy wrappers strewn all over the floor.

I scolded myself for bringing water to bed in the first place; I knew no matter how hard I tried not to, it was a given I would spill whatever liquid was within my reach. I used to joke that clumsiness was my only talent, but really, it wasn't funny.

Whenever my day started like that, which I hate to admit it often did, it became evident the day ahead wasn't going to be the best.

I pulled myself up to a sitting position and wiped my dripping hand on the old quilt-top bedspread, thinking to myself that I could have gotten a towel to clean up my mess, but then it didn't matter if I wiped my hand on my bed. No one would care anyway; no one would ever know. I was alone. I didn't even have a cat to try to hide it from if that is what cat owners would do.

I had lived alone all of my adult life, having vowed I would never share a space with anyone again once I left the comforts of my unknowingly dysfunctional parents' home. I never understood why they didn't see what I saw as I grew up. Never did they notice what my life was like; it seemed they were blind to the fact that I was such a lonely and unhappy child.

I lived by the mantra in which it was far better to be alone than to feel lonely living with others; no one could hurt me that way. Now I can't help but wonder if I had been looking at it all wrong.

I tried to push the thought of my family out of my mind and made another blind attempt for my glasses on the nightstand, hoping they had magically appeared. Unsurprisingly, they hadn't.

Frustrated by the mere fact that I couldn't see a dang thing without my spectacles, I found myself uttering nasty things to my dead parents in a sort of retaliation for giving me such horrible vision. I then questioned myself as to why I kept patting around the nightstand in vain, knowing full well I was wasting my time.

I also knew I could have saved a lot of stress if I had just turned on the light in the first place or better yet if I had used my head and thought before reaching out. If I had, I wouldn't have put my hand squarely in that wet, mushy pile of Kleenex.

In a final burst of frustration, I pushed everything from the nightstand onto the floor. Now satisfied I was smarter than the soggy mess I had made, I carefully made my way to the bedroom wall and turned on the light.

I should have just done this in the first place; with just a mere flip of the switch, the overhead light with the 100-watt bulb drenched the room with naked abandon, temporarily blinding me.

I spent a few moments with my eyes tightly closed in an attempt to save my vision from the brightness. Slowly, I opened them, squinting long enough to allow my eyes to adjust. I walked over to my nightstand, searching the floor in front of it. I had hoped that with the assistance of light, I would retrieve my precious glasses, my sweet vision, and get my day back on track. But as luck would have it, those glasses weren't anywhere to be found.

Thinking I had knocked my glasses off the nightstand, I got down on my hands and knees and began crawling around, slowly and carefully at first, then working myself up into a frenzy, to the point where I was going back and forth, sometimes just rocking on all fours. I am sure I looked like the lunatic I clearly was. I couldn't stop the words coming out of my mouth, so angry about how stupid I was. For a moment, I felt like it was my father speaking through me, mocking me. My father was much like my sister, and that did not make for a happy home.

The longer I searched, the more frustrated I became. I had only compounded that frustration by having those memories of my father taunting me as if it were some sick game. Just the thought of him raised my blood pressure; my head pulsated, threatening the possibility a migraine was on its way up and out of my eyes. I couldn't help but think of how he'd laugh at me if he saw me now.

I tried to contain myself but couldn't help getting even more frustrated with each forward motion as I searched behind the bed, under the bed, around the bed. In the midst of it, as I was asking myself how on earth I kept losing those damn things, the alarm raged its annoying call once again. I must not have shut it off.

Startled by the unexpected sound, I came up from under my bed and, in my haste, I walloped my head on the corner of the nightstand, causing me to cry out in pain. I had had enough at this point. In what could be considered well-controlled rage, I grabbed that pesky noisemaker and pulled its power cord from the wall to ensure the alarm would no longer taunt me with its constant noise.

Feeling I accomplished at least something for the first time that morning, I got back down on my knees and continued what seemed to be the never-ending search for that piece of plastic that would allow me my vision.

Going from room to room, I checked tables, counters, closets, and my purse over and over again, expecting the glasses to appear.

They didn't. After what seemed like hours of going in circles and trying to trace my steps from the night before when I still had them on, I gave up in defeat. I knew I was behind schedule and went to the bathroom to prepare for the day.

I turned on the light in the bathroom and, lo and behold, there sat my precious glasses, right where I left them the night before, sitting innocently on the bathroom counter next to a half-squeezed tube of toothpaste.

Letting out a small sigh of relief, I picked up my glasses and put them on. I felt a sense of relief now that I could see. My vision was sharp and clear once again. I scolded myself once more on my forgetfulness and then tried to focus on continuing the start of what would, unbeknownst to me, be the last day of my life.

I pulled out my old black cardigan from a pile of clothes haphazardly tossed in the corner of my bedroom – I had never been known for my housekeeping skills – and shook it out in an attempt to make it appear less wrinkled. Putting the cardigan aside, I reached for the plain white blouse with short sleeves, which showed just a hint of perspiration stains under each arm, and put it on. I followed up by putting on my long black polyester-blend skirt, which never fit quite right. It hung limply from my waist to just below my knees. Not attractive, to say the least.

I wore that outfit every day to work. It was what I called my uniform, knowing it was attire someone would more likely wear to a funeral, not for a job at the county library.

I would have preferred to wear slacks to work, as all I did was inventory books all day and box up the dusty old things to send off to some third world country where the people couldn't read them anyway.

It would have made it so much easier to wear slacks with all the climbing and lifting I had to do instead of having to keep hiking my skirt every time I went up a ladder. But there was a dress code my boss insisted I follow, so I did, in my way. I wore that outfit every day, knowing it irritated my boss to the high heavens and caused her constant requests for me to try to wear something nicer.

I wasn't out to impress her at all. Impressing bosses never got me anywhere anyway. And then there were my coworkers. It seemed all of them couldn't help looking down their noses at me like they were something far better than I; some had even gone so far as to tell me how much my lack of taste bothered them.

I thought to myself, *So what if they don't like what I wear? I am not out to impress those assholes anyway.* Really, though, it wouldn't have mattered what I had on; I still would have been criticized.

I was the butt of their jokes whenever they saw me. Don't for a moment think I didn't hear them whispering about me, mocking me for being who I was and how I looked. In my coworker's eyes, I was nothing but a clumsy, dull-looking, and moderately overweight thirty-two-year-old woman whom no one wanted. But that was nothing new; I had known that all my life. From my earliest memory, my sister made sure that fact was abundantly clear to me and anyone else around me.

I felt that way with just about everyone. I knew that, in their eyes, I did nothing but take up precious space. My peers picked up where my sister had left off, seemingly reminding me on a daily basis of how worthless I was. No one at work ever actually said this to my face, but I knew what they were all thinking, and I despised them for it.

I was not married, and even I knew there would never be a white knight on his magnificent steed just waiting to sweep me off my feet. I was nothing but that dowdy little woman with the cat-eye glasses who stammered when caught off guard by students and library patrons.

I am sure by now you can understand why there was no reason for me to try. By wearing that outfit day in and day out, it was not just my lame way of rebelling, but it also made me look like a woman in mourning because, you see, in a sense, I was.

I Died Yesterday

I put on the stockings I had found in one of my many laundry baskets of unfolded clothes and gracelessly put them on. Then I pushed a stack of papers that had taken refuge on my couch onto the floor and sat down on said couch and proceeded to put on my sensible shoes.

The shoes were equipped with Velcro strips that held them snug to my feet, instead of shoestrings. I wore those to avoid repeating the mortifying incident of when my laces came undone, causing me to trip while carrying a box of books, only to have books fly everywhere while I landed flat on the hard cement floor in the oh-so-quiet library.

Don't think for a moment I didn't hear the snickers and hushed laughter of the patrons who seemed to close in on me as I scurried around picking up books no one had looked at for years.

I vowed to myself to never let that happen again. So that night, immediately after getting off work, I went directly to the shoe store to purchase my first pair, in a long line of pairs, of Velcro shoes. Thankfully, I never had to relive that humiliating experience again.

I went to my window and pulled up the shades in the living room to let in the sunshine but was instead greeted with the bleak gray view outside my apartment window of the dirty street below me, blending into the lifeless gray sky above. The sun was deeply buried under the menacing haze of clouds, which were just waiting to pour down the buckets of rain they struggled to hold.

Hoping for some protection from the impending rain, I went to my hall closet and dug out the umbrella my sister gave me as a gift the last time I saw her, on my thirtieth birthday.

She was beaming as she handed me her gift, acting as if she was giving me the crown jewels. I was expected to be elated when I tore off the gift paper that she used to so poorly attempt to wrap the umbrella. To be honest, I was surprised she gave me a gift at all, so when she did, for a brief, fleeting moment, I felt, for the first time in a long time, somewhat happy.

But when I opened up her gift, I found it was nothing but a used, broken, lopsided excuse for an umbrella, most likely one that had been given away to some charity to avoid someone's trash bin.

I can still envision my sister, so proud of herself as she told me how she got it half off at the thrift store the day before. She couldn't even go to a regular store to find my gift.

The rain was imminent, so I decided to finally put the umbrella to use. I told myself to be grateful my sister thought of giving me a gift at all. Being I had never had an umbrella before, I figured that even if the umbrella wouldn't fully open, it just might help keep me somewhat protected from getting drenched today.

I checked the time on my wristwatch and was a little surprised to see it was just a few minutes after 7:00 a.m. I thought if I hurried, I would still be able to stop in for a quick cup of coffee at Joe's Java Hut, the little, albeit unique, coffee shop across the street from my work.

The Java Hut was heavily frequented by early morning college students trying to shake the fatigue earned by another long night of studying. Also there were the worker bees of the blue-collar class, who enjoyed the chance to mingle with the upwardly mobile white-collar crowd who sat at the small tables sprinkled around the room, talking on their phones as if they didn't have a care in the world, all the while sipping their mochas and lattes.

I knew I didn't fit in with this hodgepodge group of humanity, yet it didn't stop me from loving The Java Hut. It was the only place I could go to be both totally invisible yet feel so welcomed at the same time. I know it sounds crazy, but it's true. And it was Joe, the owner of the Java Hut, that made me feel that way. He was the kind of guy who could make anyone feel at home and who treated everyone who entered his establishment as someone of value. I admired that trait in him.

Knowing I had to hurry if I wanted to get there and not be late for work, I grabbed my purse, locked the door, and stepped out into the cold morning mist.

It had already rained quite a bit the night before, causing the streets to be wet and puddle-ridden, some with ice forming on their edges.

I felt as gray as the sky above me, but that was nothing new. Trying to shake off the bad start of the day, I walked down my rickety wooden steps, making sure to tread lightly so as not to slip and fall. I made it safely to the landing, then cautiously stepped out onto the sidewalk and walked to the curb, all the while struggling to open my precious umbrella.

I didn't notice the delivery truck that had turned the corner moments before and was coming down my street at a rate of speed that was most definitely far above the speed limit.

That truck, in its hurry to get to wherever it was going, seemed to sense my presence and veered only to hit the huge mud puddle right in front of me. The pool of water was so large I could have sworn it was the size of a small lake, as it effectively spewed dirty rainwater all over me.

I looked at myself in disbelief, up and down, then at the truck as it unapologetically drove off without a shred of concern about what it had just done to me.

My cardigan and skirt were both wet and covered with splotches of mud. It was then I felt my blood pressure soar, much like when you go to the carnival and try to hit the bell with a huge hammer to win a prize. And when that truck drenched me, it hit the spot dead on, the bell rang loudly; ding, ding, ding in my head. I could feel the vein in my temple pulsate with wild abandon.

I knew I wasn't supposed to let things get to me and I was expected to watch my blood pressure, but hell, it seemed like that truck was on a mission and had done its duty in completely ruining my day when it seemingly made me its prize.

Shaking in anger, I took in a few deep breaths in an attempt to calm myself as I pondered what to do. Defeated, I knew I didn't have another clean skirt to put on, but even if I had, I wouldn't have had the time to go back and change.

Since I didn't have the time go back to my dingy apartment and pull out something clean to wear, I did the next best thing. I looked up to the never-ending gray dampness of the sky, struggling to control my anger while cursing a God I didn't believe in for giving me such a horrible day, such a terrible life. *Why God? Oh, why me?*

I pled to the storming sky as my pulse continued to beat like a drum in my head. *What did I ever do to deserve this lousy, horrible existence?*

I don't know why I bothered since there wasn't a God to hear me anyway. Just the thought of a God was ridiculous. Resigned to the fact I could do nothing about my dilemma, I decided to continue on with my day, the dirty, wet, and soggy mess that I was. Maybe it sounds bad, but I couldn't help but take a little comfort in knowing that while it would be uncomfortable for me, it would surely bother everyone around me. I decided I would sit in everyone's work chair as soon as I got there, watching the disdain on their faces when they saw me doing so; a smile played on my face at the thought of it.

The winds were blowing, causing the air to bring a chill to the very depths of my body. More than ever, I knew I had to go to Joe's before work no matter how I looked. I had to get that damn delicious cup of coffee Joe made to bring some warmth to my insides.

The brisk wind was blowing strongly as my teeth chattered uncontrollably. I pulled my cardigan tight to my body in an attempt to block the evil wind that caused the wet clothes to chill me to the bone.

I continued my trek, walking the eight blocks to Joe's when the sky seemingly opened up and began to pour down buckets of rain on me, with drops the size of dimes pelting me, showing no mercy.

I attempted in vain to open the umbrella for protection, only to find it useless. I couldn't help but turn my face up to the heavens once again and, this time, not caring who could hear me, shout out loud, *Enough already!*

I threw the despicable umbrella in a nearby trashcan and thanked my sister out loud for caring so much about me that she so thoughtfully gave me garbage for my birthday.

I must have looked like a lunatic going on like that, but I couldn't help it and nor did I care. The day was already wrong in so many ways.

I remember how it had crossed my mind how the morning was truly a reflection of my entire life. I couldn't help but wonder why. Why did it have to continue going on that way? Knowing I wouldn't get an answer, I kept on muttering to myself until I reached the coffee shop door.

Chapter Four

What a sight I must have been when I finally made it to Joe's Java Cup. Surely I must have looked like a wild woman, with hair dripping, glasses fogged, mascara running, and clothes entirely drenched. To make matters worse, when I opened the door, I was met by what seemed the wide-eyed stares of early morning customers looking at me as if they saw a monster.

I have to say, even though I expected them to do so, I was immediately annoyed by their mere presence. I gave a woman with perfect hair and a perfect smile my best scowl, then purposefully turned my nose to the scent of coffee beans freshly ground, along with the tantalizing aroma of the fresh rolls Joe had baked earlier in the morning.

Though the morning coffee connoisseurs made me feel less than good about myself each time I came, the feeling soon dissipated when I went to the counter to order my usual.

It would be fair to say the coffee shop was the highlight of my day. No matter what the weather or if I had to go to work or if it was a Saturday morning, I would go out of my way to be there when the doors opened. I would have the first pick of the thick, gooey cinnamon caramel rolls, the size of a giant's hand, with the sweet, sugary scent. They seemed to beckon me in, enticing me to just have one delectable taste of heaven, while seducing me to dunk one into my dark roast coffee.

For the first time all morning, I could feel my spirits lift a little. It was my happy place. No wonder I died there.

I scanned the room and found a table next to the window. Not wanting to share it, as I despise morning chatter, I laid claim to it by placing my purse dead center of the table. After another quick look around, I found myself amazed that I had a table to myself at this time of the morning, considering how busy it was.

Pushing the waterlogged hair out of my eyes, I took off my cardigan and gave it good shake, this time to shed some water from it. Once done, I carefully hung it on the back of the chair that sat closest to the wall.

I could not help but notice the woman at the table in front of me with what I can only describe as a look of disgust on her face. Maybe it was because I may have gotten her a little wet from shaking out my cardigan. I shrugged off her glare and gave the woman a menacing stare until she turned away.

It was because of people like her I preferred sitting with my back to the wall whenever I was in public; it made me feel more secure in knowing no one was behind me, mocking me or observing me as if I were someone from a carnival freak show.

Once situated, I went to the counter to place my order. My heart skipped a beat when Joe himself came to the register to help me. I know I haven't mentioned this before, but I had a liking for him. Joe was not an attractive man by any means. Balding and extremely overweight with his large bulbous nose seemingly hanging from the middle of his round face made him look almost frightening, but when he smiled, he could light up a room like no other.

And it seemed he always had a smile on that mishmash face of his and was sure to use it each time he greeted me. It almost made me feel like he understood me; he'd wink at me with a puffy brown eye as if we had a secret no one else knew. I had liked to pretend we were the best of friends even though we had never had a real conversation. Joe probably never knew he was the only person in my dull, drab existence who made me feel, well, I was part of something special – if even for a moment.

I admired his dedication, how he would get up long before the rest of the world and come to this little shop to bake those delectable treats that were proudly displayed in his pristine showcases each and every morning, seven days a week. His baking was an art, and my stomach thanked him for it every chance it could.

It was if Joe knew me. I never had to tell him what I wanted when I went to order. With a wink and a smile, he would have my roll and coffee, robust and steaming hot, waiting for me at the counter when he saw me come in. Today was much the same, but he surprised me this time. I was prepared to pay him when he stopped me and said that today's purchase was on him. No one but him was ever that kind to me. I thought to myself maybe it wasn't going to be such a bad day after all. As he stood there smiling at me, I felt my face grow hot as I blushed and I stammered a meek thank you, after which I quickly took my seat and looked out the window so Joe wouldn't see my face as I smiled. I noticed the rain continuing to beat down, pelting the window with deliberation, as if it meant to shatter that glass and soak everyone who dared to even be near it.

But at that moment, it didn't matter to me if it happened or not. Joe, with his funny face and misshapen body, had given me a roll and coffee for no reason. And that made me feel good. Too bad I never got to eat that roll.

Chapter Five

Sipping on the steaming cup of coffee that held the java I adored, I took in the café around me. At first glance, you would think you were in an up north cabin type lodge or more definitely a man cave, rather than an urban coffee shop. Joe had decorated the place in man cave style, with bobble head baseball and football players lining one wall, just high enough that people could still see them but not steal them. He proudly displayed his trophies from his hunting trips, showcasing a deer head with massive antlers, surrounded by fish of every size and color and other animals with names I couldn't recall. Joe liked to tell the story of how he got the big buck, the most monstrous creature he'd ever seen, and that he got it on the first shot, right in the heart. Rumor had it that the deer had met its demise when hit by a semi and that Joe had found it on the side of the road, but I chose to believe Joe.

Joe was an avid bowler and was most proud of his talent at the bowling lanes. Right on top of his donut counter, he displayed his trophies, and there were a lot of them, all neatly organized by the date he had won them. It seemed a little silly to me; maybe it was because I had never won anything. Those trophies were as, if not more, sacred as his bobble heads. Everyone who knew Joe knew if you were to even put the finger on one of them, Joe would give you a piece of his mind. A few years ago, someone did, and after the way Joe reacted, no one was brave enough to put their hands on them again.

The delectable scent of coffee and fresh-from-the-oven rolls surely didn't fit in this environment, but maybe that is what made the Java Cup so charming. I knew there was nowhere else I would rather be.

Looking once more out the window, I observed people briskly walking down the sidewalk, some in groups, some alone, with umbrellas that worked correctly, their heads down, fighting what seemed to be nearly a losing battle to the wind, to get to wherever their destination was that morning. Horns were blowing, people were talking on their phones, a dog was barking insanely as his master took him for his morning walk, a woman stopped to apply what looked like another layer of lipstick on an already well-coated mouth. Everyone seemed to have such a purpose. *Everyone but me.*

I turned my attention back to my cinnamon roll and told myself my only purpose was to eat the warm, delicious specimen of bakery goods before it got cold.

I was about to do so when I noticed the table next to mine had just become available and that whoever had been there moments before left behind a newspaper.

I put down my yet-to-be-eaten cinnamon bun and quickly jumped up to claim the paper for my own. Glancing around much like a mouse would when looking out for prey to assure myself no one had noticed my actions, I thought briefly how silly that might have looked. I don't know why I even bothered, though; I knew not one of the customers noticed I was even there in the first place. Everyone was too busy doing whatever it was they were doing to notice me, yet as I snatched up the paper and quickly returned to my seat, I took one more look around the room to see if anyone cared.

The clock on the wall next to the door showed the time to be three minutes to 8:00 a.m. Even after the fiasco that started my morning, I was pleased to see I had at least another fifteen minutes before I had to leave there to get to work, allowing me plenty of time to read the paper to see what was happening in the world.

Not that I cared, mind you. The world was a dark, nasty place run by rules no one followed. But for that moment, it gave me something to do that would make me look like I too belonged there.

As I opened the paper, I felt a slight twinge on the left side of my body. It lasted only a moment and, once it passed, I put it off that maybe I had pulled a muscle when I was crawling around like a child on a mission earlier that morning. It was nothing. Or so I thought.

Finding it hard to read the paper, I took off my glasses and proceeded to wipe the spots of rain that had covered them. Once satisfied, I again began to read the discarded paper. I scanned over an article about human rights and thought of how ironic that term was. What rights did anyone truly have? The cards were stacked against all of us, most especially me. No one was going to respect my human rights. Our world was damned.

After mentally tearing apart the absurdity of what the writer was trying to convince the world of, I turned to the entertainment section of the paper, hoping to find something interesting there.

Once again, I felt that odd twinge on my left side, this time spreading to just above my heart. The feeling lasted longer and was stronger, somewhat painful, enough so to cause me to gasp for breath. It stopped again, and for a moment, I thought I must have been experiencing heartburn from the chili I had for dinner the night before. Another twinge, stronger this time, and again it subsided. I found it odd that indigestion could come and go like that.

Within seconds, the next twinge went from a twinge to sheer and utter pain. Now concerned, I put down the paper, perplexed at what I felt my body do. In short order, the pain subsided again, and I wondered to myself if perhaps I was overreacting. Maybe all I was experiencing really was heartburn from the chili I ate for dinner the night before. I took a deep breath, vowing never to eat chili again.

I decided to stop and get Rolaids after leaving the café, and if I were late getting to work, it was just too damn bad. My heartburn came first.

My mother always said I had a flair for the dramatic and that I had a talent of blowing the simplest of things out of proportion. Maybe she was right, and my imagination was feeding into things. Feeling somewhat satisfied with my decision I, for a brief moment, pondered whether I lived my whole life blowing things out of proportion.

After deciding my mother was wrong on how I viewed the world, I pushed her out of my thoughts and reached for my coffee cup.

When I picked up the cup, I was overcome with a pain so intense, it jarred me as it radiated through my chest and down my left arm. The pain was so excruciating and inexplicable; I had never felt such agony in my life.

I screamed. It was a scream so guttural, it jolted my senses. The coffee cup I held in my hand flew upward and spilled hot coffee down the front of me. I felt my skin burn from the hot liquid. But none of that mattered. I felt as if an elephant was standing on my chest and the only thing I could do was focus on the tearing, sheer agony that had spread up and down the left side of my chest.

By this point, I realized this was not my imagination at work. My mind went into overdrive, compelling me to try to get help. I grabbed the table for support in an attempt to lift myself out of my seat, and as I did, I remember an even stronger pain ripped through me.

I had never felt anything like this; the pain was so intense, so horrendous, it caused my knees to buckle beneath me. I fell face down on the floor, in pure and utter agony.

In vain, I tried to cry out for help, but not a sound came out of my mouth. I remember an overwhelming feeling of loss come over me. At this point, I was beginning to fear for my life.

I looked up at the wall clock once again. It was now 8:02 a.m. I thought to myself in irony, *Looks like I won't make it in to work after all*. Then it hit me. I realized something bigger was at hand. *Oh no, oh dear, oh my God, am I dying?* Then my life as I knew it went dark.

Chapter Six

There I was, a sight to see. My body sprawled on the coffee shop floor, legs spread eagle in the most unflattering way. My arms were thrown on either side of my body as if I were about to fly. But what was most frightening to observe, I saw that my head was turned to the side with my eyes open, seemingly staring into the abyss. I noticed I no longer felt any pain, which I thought curious. I remember thinking I just had a heart attack, but if I did, why had the pain stopped? I thought the episode had passed and everything would be okay.

Again, I looked down on that body, lying like a discarded rag doll on the hard checkered linoleum, confused by what I saw. I tried to understand what I was seeing and then it occurred to me that the body on the floor was me. What I was looking *at* really was me. In a panic, I wondered why I wasn't moving. Then it hit me; it was because I was looking at my dying or already dead body. But how was that possible? I was too young to die!

Apparently, I must have landed with quite a thud, causing the patrons in the coffee shop to stop whatever they were doing so they could gawk at my seemingly lifeless form. The room became eerily quiet except for the sound of cups hitting their saucers, of chairs scraping against the linoleum as people turned to get a better look at the excitement happening before them, and the quiet murmurs asking one another what had happened.

For a brief moment, I thought to myself*, Great, now you notice me*, but I really couldn't blame them; I too was staring at the limp form of myself lying there, unmoving, wondering what the hell just happened.

I don't know if I can explain the emotions I experienced at that moment, but I will try. To say I was confused would have been an understatement, as it didn't make sense that I was apparently floating above everyone, watching what was unfolding below me as if it weren't happening to me.

I had the same vantage point as the massive deer head, seven feet off the ground and, like that head, I was no longer a part of the life happening below.

Suddenly, the room came alive with movement. I watched the woman, who, with her perfect hair, nails, makeup, and wearing her designer clothes, as she screamed for someone to call 911. She was hysterical, shouting over and over, "This woman is having a heart attack or a seizure or something. Someone do something now. Oh my God!"

Honestly, I was in shock at this point. It was unbelievable to see myself on that floor, with my mouth wide open, eyes rolling back into my head, and my now uncontrollably jerking body as it experienced the throes of my life-ending heart attack.

In what seemed within less than a second, Joe came rushing from behind the counter, ordering people to stop staring at me and move aside. Joe came to my heaving body and knelt down on the floor next to me. His thick frame seemed to crumple as he raised my head and looked into my eyes.

Joe tried to comfort my nearly lifeless, jerking body, telling me over and over everything would be okay, that I would be okay. Without taking his eyes off me, Joe shouted for someone, anyone to go in the back and get the Automatic External Defibrillator machine.

As the patrons crowded in closer, each hoping to catch a glimpse of the action, Joe gently laid my head on a towel he had pulled from his waistband, then started CPR.

As I watched, he blew into my mouth. I began to panic when I realized that even though I saw Joe blowing air into my lungs, it didn't do anything. I was already blue from lack of oxygen at this point. I willed Joe to breathe deeper, blow harder, make my lungs work, whatever he had to do, to bring me back. I watched as he repeated the steps: breathe into my mouth, compress my chest, listen for a heartbeat; he made those motions over and over. His attempt to save me seemed to go on for hours, but, in retrospect, I think it was more like a minute or two. By then, I saw a man, thin and lanky and sporting a pencil-thin mustache, push through the onlookers as he ordered them to move out of the way.

I knew this man, not by the name of course, but by sight. He came to the café nearly every morning, and whenever he cast his eyes upon me, he never failed to make me feel I was beneath him. Now, though, his look changed to compassion as he made his way through the crowd. He was stern in his tone as he said, "Move and let me through. I am a doctor; I can help. Just let me through."

When the doctor reached me, he knelt down by my side and softly spoke to Joe. "Joe, you need to let me take over from here. I can help her."

Joe looked up at him with tears in his eyes. "You really can help her, right?"

The doctor replied softly, "I'm going to try my best, Joe." The doctor looked over his shoulder and said, "I need towels; someone bring me some towels! And has anyone called 911?" A voice responded from the back, saying paramedics were on the way.

The doctor turned back to my body, then unbuttoned my coffee-stained white blouse. He opened it wide as he asked for scissors to cut my bra off. In a flash, it seemed the doctor had magically acquired the scissor he requested, and with two quick cuts, my bra was no longer covering my chest. Even though I was most likely completely dead by then, I was mortified at seeing my breasts exposed to the world. I looked from my body to the group of onlookers, expecting to hear someone make some snide comment about my lack of endowment, but thankfully, I didn't hear anyone say a word.

A woman bowed her head and began praying for me. I was touched by her action as no one had ever done that for me before. Now no longer concerned about being exposed, I felt a spark of hopefulness that maybe her prayers would be answered, and I was going to be okay.

Just then, the employee Joe had sent to the back came out, holding a defibrillator. The doctor took the machine from the employee's hands and began preparing it to use on me.

Visibly shaken, Joe slid over to the other side of my body, never once taking his hand off of me. His concern touched me; I was surprised to see the steady stream of tears running down his face onto mine.

Joe was genuinely afraid that I was dying. His concern took me aback. Why would he be crying over me? I had no idea he cared so much about me. I willed my mouth to move so I could tell him I was okay, that I wasn't hurting, but try as I did, my body refused to cooperate.

The doctor adjusted the defibrillator settings and then picked the paddles up, readying himself to place them on my bare, exposed chest. The doctor told Joe not to touch me as he put the paddles on my chest.

Joe was sobbing by this point as he continued talking to me, telling me to stay strong; everything was going to be okay.

I was in awe, so moved by his concern for me. I wanted to thank him for thinking I was worth his tears.

At that moment, so many thoughts, so many emotions hit me; so quickly and all at once, like a rocket, my emotions soared. Then, just as quickly, the reality of what had happened jolted me down to the deepest of depths.

There is no way to explain what it feels like when you realize your life is over; no matter what, you can't change anything. You are never going to live again.

All I could think was how unfair it all was. Why me? Why had my life, my world ended like this? I was too young to die! For God's sake, I hadn't even lived yet. My life had never been fair, and now I was dead at just thirty-two years old? It was all so unfair. I never got to experience my first love or have children or anything I had wanted. I hadn't lived the life I wanted; the person who lived in my body was not who I was. God, no! If I had known the life I had was going to end like this, I would have…I would have…I don't know what I would have done, but it certainly wouldn't end like this. Regret poured from the depths of my soul.

It was not fair that I hadn't lived my life. The life I got wasn't something to be enjoyed; rather, it was something I was forced to endure. Never in my miserable existence had I stopped to think life could have been different, that it could have been good, beautiful, and whole. Why had I never even tried to live any other way than what I had? What the hell was wrong with me?

I tried to forgive myself for the way I lived. It wasn't my fault life had been horrible. I couldn't have changed something that I never had a chance at in the first place. It was their fault, those people in my life who sucked any chance of happiness out of my existence. My sister, my boss, anyone who ever crossed my path; they are the ones that created the miserable, bitter woman I was.

I was lying on a cold, linoleum floor, like a broken rag doll, as I watched my body jolt upwards each time the doctor yelled "clear" and put the paddles to my chest. I mourned the loss of what could have been every time my body fell back to the floor in a lifeless heap. Defeat overwhelmed me. It was clear I was never going to have the life I deserved.

Anger welled up in my soul, anger as hungry as a wolf, waiting impatiently to devour me. The anger was uncontrollable as I thought about how I never got the chance to live my life. I wanted to lash out at the world that created the monster that was me. But I couldn't because I was dead.

I was appalled at what I saw when I again looked down at the people who surrounded me. They reminded me of vultures as they circled to get a better look at the shell of what used to be me. I wanted to tell them to stop staring at me, to get the hell away from me. The doctor had given up on the defibrillator when the paramedics arrived and pronounced me dead as they set up the gurney to haul out my body.

Some onlookers spoke in hushed tones, asking each other what happened. Was it because they cared? No, it was because they wanted more information about their upcoming gossip session, of that I was sure.

My heart ached, metaphorically, of course. Though my heart had stopped, my soul felt every ounce of despair knowing this was it. I was dead.

As the paramedics spoke with the doctor who had tried in vain to save me, I noticed a man, likely my age, in his early thirties with dirty blonde hair, wearing a goofy smile on his face as he took picture after picture of my dead body. How dare he do such a thing? The bitterness I felt was tangible. With everything my bodiless soul had to give, I shouted at him, "Put your damn camera down! I hate you all! You people deserved this so much more than I ever did! I was not ready to die, not now; no, not now!"

I turned my attention to the darkness, pleading to the very God I didn't believe in, "Please, this was all a mistake. If you do exist, if you are out really there, then please, God, please, give me another chance!" My soul shouted with a voice that was no longer a voice, to an entity who, if he existed, had no interest in hearing me.

Then I saw a young boy, all of about five years old with his mouth agape as he stood next to my left, twisted leg. It was evident the boy was concerned about the sight in front of him.

He turned his head and looked up at his mother as he repeatedly tugged on her pants leg in a seemingly futile attempt to get her attention. He pulled once more on her pants leg, this time with more urgency. "Mommy, Mommy, what happened to her?" Ironically, I thought, *That's a good question.* What was going on here? This whole experience simply could not be real.

The little boy's voice must have sounded alarming enough to snap his mother out of her grotesque trance, causing her to stop ogling my limp body as she looked down at him. He had tears in his eyes.

His mother knelt down to his level and questioned her son, "Frankie, what is the matter?"

I thought to myself, *Is that lady serious? Asking her son what was wrong, when the thing that was obviously wrong was blue on the café floor. Someone should call child protection on her!*

The boy, clearly shaken, told her he was scared about what he had witnessed. I nodded my bodiless head, understanding him completely. Of course he was afraid! What child wouldn't be? I was astounded to hear this pitiful excuse for a mother tell her son never to mind, the lady on the floor was just sleeping, and not to worry.

How could she say I was just sleeping and everything was fine? How dare she lie to him like that?

Hopefully, it was because she suddenly realized what a horrible mother she was to allow her son to witness my dead body that caused her to decide it would be a good time to leave. I nearly forgave her as she took hold of the little boy's hand and led him away, not realizing she was digging in her purse with her other hand to find her cell phone.

She found it in short order and immediately began pushing numbers. As she held the phone to her ear, I heard her say, in only what could be described as morbid excitement, "Oh Marge, you are not going to believe what happened just now. I told you should have come with me this morning. See, there was this woman; she stood up looking all white and pasty – well, I saw her take a step, then watched her as she keeled over, right in front of us!" She said it with the kind of enthusiasm someone who might have won the lottery might have; she sounded almost giddy, for God's sake! The woman stopped talking long enough to listen to her friend's response, then continued talking to her friend, telling her all about her story, which was my story, a story she had no right to share. If I had hands that worked, I would have strangled her for being so morbid.

"Yeah, she did. I am sure she's dead." Just to make sure, the mother of the year stopped abruptly, which caused her little boy to do an about face. She turned around to get a better view of what was happening and continued, "Or at least I think she's dead! She must be, I mean, she's foaming at the mouth and turning blue! And paramedics and cops are everywhere! I tell you, Marge, it's like a circus here. The only thing missing is the popcorn! Can you come down? You have got to see this!"

Disgusted, I moved my essence as close to her as possible, hoping she would feel my presence as I screamed into her ear, "You pathetic excuse for a human being, your friend does not have to see this! What the hell is wrong with you? How dare you tell your friend she should have seen me die?"

The woman clearly hadn't heard me; she never even blinked as I tried to crawl into her head and make her listen. Why would she call someone and say such a thing? She didn't seem to realize my death wasn't some free freak show. But the worst part of it all? Letting her little boy witness my body as it as it convulsed and not thinking twice about the nightmares he might have after seeing my skin turn blue.

I felt crazed as a dam of emotion burst from within me; it was the very dam I had emotionally built so I wouldn't have to feel. But now I felt every emotion I had bottled up my entire life, twisting my soul with the strength of a tornado, spinning me around and around as I wailed in utter agony over my death.

I had never felt such mourning, not even when my parents died or when my grandparents died. The pain was all so new to me, so much so I can't even begin to describe it to you as I still can't comprehend it.

I was mourning for myself, of course; me, the pathetic woman who died with the audience I never wanted, getting attention I never wanted. The finality of my death was gut wrenching, as I saw what I once was, no longer having any real meaning. With a certain coldness, the paramedics lifted me up and placed my body into a black body bag, then zipped it from head to toe. The attendants put me on the gurney, clearly not having a good grip on my body as the paramedic who lifted the top portion of my body seemed to slip on something. Thank God he didn't drop me.

I thought I could stand no more, but somehow, like anyone who witnesses a tragedy; I continued to watch the events playing out before me. I struggled to understand why the people in the café that day seemed to feed like vultures on the sight of my dead body. I wondered if I wouldn't have done the same. But I knew for certain I wouldn't have stayed for the show; it wasn't my thing. But for those despicable monsters who wanted to see how it all played out, it gave them something to talk about at the dinner table tonight. They seemed frozen where they stood.

I cried out to them, realizing the futility of it, but for my sake had to say something. "Please don't talk about me; I have never liked anyone speaking about me." If anyone heard, no one listened.

I found myself lost and confused at what I was experiencing. I questioned everything that had just transpired. I told myself none of this was real; I rationalized that maybe I had just fainted or this was all just a terrible dream. I mean, if I had indeed died, where then was the bright light everyone talked about seeing after you died?

Not only was there no light waiting for me, but there were also no loved ones standing there just ahead with arms wide open for me to join them in paradise.

Convinced what I experienced was just a nightmare I couldn't wake up from, my brain searched for answers.

Deep down, though, I knew something was not right. I couldn't see anything, but I sure as hell felt something. An epic amount of rage ran through my soul, fueled by the injustice I felt toward the very people who made me who I was. And to be honest, it seemed everyone who crossed my path seemed to do me wrong.

I turned my attention back to the activity in the café. I heard someone say, "Show is over, folks. Let the paramedics through."

With those words, like a sea parting, the gawkers moved out of the way, letting the paramedics wheel my lifeless body through them and out the door, which for me sealed my fate. All hope for it being a nightmare ended. I was dead.

Moments after my anticlimactic departure of the café, I watched as the gawkers trailed behind the paramedics, like they were in a macabre parade, talking in hushed tones to one another about what they had witnessed.

I thought sarcastically, *My, my, what a day it has been for them. Those people saw a life end and then went on with their days, their lives, trying in vain to not sound excited when telling anyone who would listen what they had witnessed.*

The café was empty within moments, with only one person remaining. And that was Joe. He stood in the middle of the room, surrounded by empty tables and half eaten pastries, looking down at where my body had lain only moments before. My soul felt a tinge of regret of dying there when I realized Joe was still crying. I was so touched by his emotion and questioned myself as to why had I never noticed how much he had cared about me? How could I have been I so blind?

With tears still streaming down his face, Joe made his way to the front door and turned the open sign on the glass door to closed, not wanting any more customers that morning.

A man stood outside in the rain with a frown on his face as he waved his hand, trying to get Joe's attention. Joe didn't notice him as he locked the front door. The man began frantically pounding on the door, his voice rising as he demanded to come in, but it was to no avail. Joe turned from the door and walked away with his head hung low.

Joe reached for the light switch on the wall and shut the lights off in his now lifeless business, then disappeared out the back door, no longer wanting to be there himself.

I couldn't believe Joe closed his shop because of me. It was evident he was mourning my death. If only I had known I had such an effect on this man, I could only imagine how different my life might have been.

Chapter Seven

I mentioned earlier that once you die, time has no meaning. Days may be mere minutes, seconds could be years, and hours mean nothing, yet moments mean everything.

I had no idea where I was or how long I had been here. The fear I had was overwhelming. I saw nothing but the never-ending blackness that held my soul captive. I was all alone, so alone, in a darkness so thick, it was smothering. I felt the darkness as it wrapped itself tightly around me, cutting deep into my soul, touching the very core of my existence.

You see, even though my body had expired, my soul continued. It continued into a darkness where there was no warmth, only bleakness, menacing in its nature.

I clearly was nowhere near the mythical place called heaven you read about in children's books. There were no pearly gates, no angels, nothing at all.

But inexplicably, I knew I wasn't alone. I felt the evil that surrounded me, licking its cold lips as if waiting impatiently to devour me.

I don't know how long I was in that black hole of cold darkness; it may have just been moments yet seemed as if I had been there forever. But really, however long I was in that state of limbo didn't matter; either way, it was much too long.

Trying to gather myself, I heard my disembodied voice as I pled to the darkness, "Please, tell me why am I here! Tell me, what does all of this mean?'

It felt as if, with every moment, the evil moved closer to me, encompassing me as I cried out to the darkness, "Why me? Was I such a bad person that now this is how it ends?" No response was given, only the deafening silence around me.

No matter how hard I tried to make sense of what was happening, no answer was given. In vain, I, with the bodiless eyes of my soul, struggled to see what it was around me, in the hope once I knew, once I understood, that the darkness would lift.

As I struggled to find an answer, I noticed a grayness moving in from nowhere yet everywhere around me. I briefly felt a sense of hope, but immediately realized I shouldn't have. As I struggled to adjust to the shift from black to gray, I noticed I could smell something familiar. The odor was dreadfully familiar.

The stench of stale beer and cigarette smoke began to overwhelm me. The stronger the smell became, the more wretched it was; it taunted me with its familiarity. I could not move away from the horrible smell; I was forced to let it touch me, embedding its odor into my soul. As this was happening, I noted the patch of gray became larger and lighter, until it was nearly transparent.

It was then I was bewildered to see my sister in front of me. Had she died and come to me? No, I soon realized she wasn't there with me at all. I was in her kitchen with her.

There she was; my dear sister sat in all her glory, wearing a dirty, ragged robe that may have been white at one time, but now looked to be a dullish gray color. I couldn't help but notice her hair was an unruly mess; most likely due to the fact that a hairbrush hadn't touched it in days, if not weeks.

Though I had chosen to not see my sister over the past few years, I couldn't help checking her out from head to toe, hoping I would notice if anything positive had changed with her, but nothing had.

The years had not been kind when it came to aging. Though only forty-two years old, my sister could have easily passed for someone decades older. The wrinkles on her forehead and around her eyes belied the look of someone her age.

The permanent scowl, which had been sketched on her face since childhood, had deepened even more, now literally pulling her lips down, as if her mouth had gravity fighting any chance of a smile to cross her face. The lines between her mouth and chin resembled that of a ventriloquist's dummy.

Her eyes were mere slits in her head, open just enough for me to see the pupils dilated, most likely from the prescription pain medication she liked to take whenever she could talk a doctor into prescribing it for her.

I did my best not to notice her hygiene but found it impossible, as it was worse than ever. God only knew when the last time was she bathed or even washed her hair. My sister reeked of old food, stale cigarettes, and her constant companion, beer.

My sister was a large woman who seemed to have only grown larger since I last saw her. She sat perched on an old wobbly wooden kitchen chair that had one leg seemingly held in place by duct tape, straining to hold her ever-expanding girth.

The kitchen was dingy and dank. I am sure sunlight hadn't visited that room in years as the curtains were not merely closed, but safety-pinned shut in her attempt to keep the world out.

The old Formica table that sat in the center of the kitchen doubled as her computer desk. She didn't seem to mind the cluttered table, strewn with countless empty beer bottles.

It was as if those bottles were her private sentinels, building her wall to oblivion as she drowned herself in beer each and every night. My mother would have been shocked to see her this way. The disgust I had for her brewed up within me.

She seemed frozen as she sat in front of the flickering computer monitor, her eyes glazed over from the beer or staring at the computer for hours or maybe a combination of both. The only movement was to flick the ash off her cigarette into the overflowing ashtray on the table or to take a swig of her beer or move the mouse.

The television flickered in the empty living room as the voices blared out from it. My sister always had the sound on as high as it could go so that she could listen to her ridiculous soap operas. She was totally obsessed with them. Whenever I had to talk to her, she spoke of the characters nonstop, as if she knew them personally.

The wall phone in the kitchen began ringing incessantly, but my sister made no attempt to answer it; it was almost as if the fog she was in couldn't be penetrated.

She couldn't have known that on the other end of the phone was a morgue attendant who was trying to find my next of kin. I imagine it's one of the hardest parts of the job, having to pick up the phone to notify someone about the loss of a loved one.

After what felt like forever, she snapped out of her trance, highly irritated someone had the gall to disturb her. My sister made her way across the kitchen, in slow, deliberate steps to avoid falling, and finally answered the phone.

Clearly irritated by the interruption, she answered the phone, her voice crass, as if to let the caller know she was being bothered in the most inconvenient way. "Hello? Who's calling me at this hour?"

The morgue attendant, taken aback by her tone, took a deep breath and said, "I am looking for the parents of Terese Manning."

My sister's interest piqued. "Well, you can stop looking. My parents died years ago." She paused for a brief moment, then continued, "Why do you want them anyway? Is Terese in trouble? Wouldn't surprise me, the worthless piece of crap she is."

Struggling to keep his voice calm, the morgue attendant replied, "No, no, ma'am, she is not in any trouble at all."

She spat into the phone, "Then why in the hell are you bothering me? I was in the middle of something."

"Well, I'm calling from the county morgue and, well, the reason I'm calling is that, um, I have bad news. I need to inform you your sister has had a fatal heart attack."

"How fatal is she? You mean like dead fatal?" Her voice slurred as she cradled the phone and walked to the refrigerator for her next, but certainly not last, beer of the night.

The morgue attendant was shocked at the question. But my sister wasn't done with what she had to say. She continued, "If this is a joke, it's not a funny one. I have half a mind to end this nonsense and hang up this damn phone right now!"

The morgue attendant couldn't believe what he was hearing, but I could. Ah, my dear, sweet sister. There she goes again, always thinking of me, but never in the right way.

Incredulously the morgue attendant continued, "I'm sorry to have to tell you this way, but we need you to come down to the morgue and make arrangements."

My sister scoffed, "What arrangements? I haven't spoken to my sister in years, and now I'm supposed to come and take care of her business? Well, let me tell you, sir, I am glad she is dead. Good riddance to bad rubbish, I say."

The morgue attendant couldn't comprehend the coldness of this woman on the other end of the line. Barely able to contain himself, he replied, "Well, yes, ma'am. But you are her next of kin, you are her sister, and it's the family's, well, it's your responsibility, to, um, you do need to take care of this."

She hissed into the receiver, "Nope, not going to; she is your problem now." With that, she slammed down the phone as hard as she could.

I watched her as she spoke out loud to herself. "Next of kin, my ass! Sure hope she had some life insurance for her dear sister." My sister returned to her computer, muttering under her breath, then lit a cigarette and resumed her trance. I saw once and for all that I did not matter to her.

Why in God's name did I have to witness this? What the hell is going on? My sister had always been the very bane of my existence. She was ten years older than me and was just plain mean; I don't remember a time she wasn't that way.

My sister had been an only child for the first ten years of her life. When my mother became pregnant with me, my sister was excited at the thought of having a little brother. My mom told me my sister would kiss her stomach every day and say, "How are you in there, little brother? I just can't wait to meet you!"

It never occurred to her there might be a little girl in my mother's ever expanding belly. Because for her, the mere thought of having a little sister was completely out of the question. My sister was the princess, and she was not about to share her title with anyone.

Once my sister learned about my birth, she locked herself in her bedroom and refused to speak to my mother for at least the week. In her ten-year-old mind, she believed my parents must have decided she wasn't good enough, so they went out and got a new little girl and not the little brother that she always wanted. And for that, I paid.

The earliest memory of my sister was when I was about three years old. Due to a speech impediment, I often struggled with my words.

I knew that there had been something wrong because even though I knew what I was saying, I would have to repeat myself to others over and over.

My sister found pleasure in my inability to speak properly. She loved seeing something wrong with me. My sister was then thirteen years old and I just three years old. I remember I had been afraid of her even then, and as a child, I was always apprehensive talking in front of her. She'd "repeat" whatever I had said in gibberish. She would say she was merely repeating what I said, but even at that young age, I knew she was mocking me, making fun of me. Sometimes she would torment me to the point of tears. But that was just what she had hoped for, so whenever I cried, she laughed. If I threatened to tell our parents of her treatment of me, she threatened me back, telling me she'd do horrible things to me. I couldn't win.

That might not seem like much, but she was my big sister. Wasn't she supposed to look out for me, protect me, *love* me?

The worst time of the day was bedtime. My sister and I had to share a bed, and that bed was a place where nightmares came true for me.

My sister had me thoroughly convinced there were monsters under the bed, just waiting to get me when the lights went out. She would do whatever she could to make bedtime hell. She would hit me, kick me, punch me, pull my hair, call me names, and push me off the bed; literally anything she could do to make me cry. My sister thrived on hurting me. I now believe she was taking all of her remaining anger of the day and giving it to me full force.

She plotted against me and did sick things to me. There was the time my sister spent an entire day picking her nose and wiping it on my favorite pillow. Clearly, she was determined to get me good that night. By nightfall, the bottom of my favorite pillow had been thoroughly encrusted by her waste.

I can't tell you how excited my sister was about me having to go to bed that night. She was pleased with what she had accomplished and could barely contain herself as she waited for me to crawl into my corner of the bed.

I should have known something was up with her. She had acted somewhat kind to me that day, something out of the norm for her.

I put on my pajamas and got into bed; the bed we shared. As I always did, I grabbed my pillow and hugged it tightly for some comfort. Sleeping with my sister was always a dread-filled time. I did whatever I could to sleep as far away from her as possible, with one leg usually hanging over the side of the bed as I rocked myself back and forth, trying to lull myself to sleep, doing my best to blot out my sister's voice as she taunted me.

The very worst part, though, was when she would touch me. I didn't want to be close enough to her to be able to put her hands on me or take my hand and make me touch her body in places I didn't want to go. It was just too much for a little girl to handle.

But back to that night. I wish I could forget how interested she was about my comfort, asking me if the pillow felt good.

I found that odd but told her my pillow was all right. She mocked my speech impediment with the words I had spoken back to me, all with a grin on her face.

She asked again if I were sure. Then, with evil in her voice, she said she wanted to know because she had done something special to it to make it just right for me. I thought that a rare act of kindness on her part and let my guard down for a moment.

I again told her my pillow was fine, then asked her what she did to make it special. Just asking caused her to break out in a fit of laughter that seemed never to end. When she finally pulled herself together, my sister told me what she had done. She was so proud of herself.

She made my childhood hell. There were those times my mother would have her watch me to give her a break; I was filled with dread every time my mom told my sister to take me with her when she went to do things with her friends. Clearly, both my mother and my father were blind to the fact that my sister lived to terrorize me.

On our little outings, my sister took great pleasure in hitting me, burn me with her cigarettes, tripping me, mocking me; whatever she could do to make me even more terrified of her. Her abuse would happen every single time my mother made my sister take me with her.

I was about eight years old when my sister took me over to the house of a friend of hers. I remember her telling me on the way there that I had better be good or I'd be in big trouble. She would make me pay.

Within moments of arriving, she locked me in a small, dark, unlit bathroom and told me there was a rat in the room. I could hear her, with just a door between us, laughing. She proceeded to get high with her other friends, not concerned with the fear she had instilled in me behind that locked bathroom door. I remember her saying if I wasn't quiet, they'd never let me out and would burn the house down. No matter how much I fought or banged on the door, no matter how loud I cried or pled to be let out, she never came to my rescue.

When the door opened, finally freeing me from that nightmare, I ran out the door in tears, and all the way home could only think of how I hated her.

After outings with her, she would grab my face, look into my eyes, and say, "If you say anything to Mom or Dad, I will kill you, you little witch." I believed her; I never said a word.

By far, her favorite thing to say to me was that I was a mistake and that my parents had never wanted me. According to her, I wasn't supposed to be born; she'd expected to have a brother. As far as she was concerned, I ruined that for her. She was a bitter, evil person.

I envied my school friends who had sisters who would braid their hair, play with them, read them stories at night. It just wasn't fair that I had to live with someone who despised me so.

The happiest day of my life was the day she ran off with some guy she had met at a bar. I was twelve years old at the time, and for the first time in my life, I felt the weight of her presence lifted off me. It was the first time I ever really felt gratitude for anything. My reprieve from her torment didn't last long however. She was only gone a few years before she came back home for good.

When I was twenty-two years old, my sister claimed she wanted to make amends and be the sister I had always wanted.

Craving a sisterly bond with her, I believed her, I thought maybe it was possible she wanted to make a difference in our relationship; I opened my heart and gave her another chance.

The thing is, even though years had passed, my sister proved in no time things hadn't changed at all; she was as demeaning and demanding as ever. I gave her my all and tried my best to create the bond sisters can have with her. It was the one thing I had always wanted, but she soon showed me that was not possible.

The final straw was the one and only time I ever went out with her. She said she'd love to go out and "get to know one another." I jumped at the opportunity.

We had gone out to have a cocktail in the small bar, the only bar, in our hometown. We knew everyone in there and shared pleasantries with the other patrons in the bar, and I felt that maybe we could be friends after all. That is, up until she slapped me across the face because a man spoke to me and not to her.

Right there, in public, out of a jealous rage, my sister, took it upon herself to open-hand slap me across the face, without any concern of who witnessed it and no concern regardless about what my reaction might be. That was the final straw; I was done trying. I got up, walked out, and vowed to never let her hurt me again.

But now, there I was, watching her play out my final insult from her. She hadn't cared less I was dead. I couldn't help but think, for maybe the thousandth time, how can someone who is supposed to be your family be so wicked? But more importantly, why was I being forced to watch her continue to do so after I died?

I wanted desperately to get out of there, get away from her and her contempt, but I couldn't. I was stuck in some limbo; being held there by a God I didn't know. I just couldn't comprehend why I was forced to witness her hate.

I could no longer stand the sight before me. I turned away from my sister and cried out into the darkness, "Why, God, why? Please, I will do anything if you'd just make this stop!"

I should have known there would not be a response; just a black empty void that no light could penetrate. Honestly, I didn't know what was worse.

It seemed I was there for several hours, watching her, sitting there, not caring one iota about me. Why on earth would this person who never wanted me at all be the same someone my soul would be forced to observe? I hoped this wasn't what my eternity was going to be, because I knew this to be my own personal hell.

I heard something from a distance, something behind me. It felt like a whisper, yet no words were spoken.

I don't know how I knew that whisper was meant for my ears only. Once again, I heard the voice and struggled to decipher what was being said to me. I turned to the direction the whisper seemed to be coming from, leaning into the darkness, struggling to hear the voice from the abyss when I finally heard what it was telling me.

I thought I must have heard wrong and strained, even more, to understand better what was being said. What the voice was telling me was the most absurd thing I had ever heard. This entity, whoever was speaking to me, wanted me to do the unthinkable.

This soundless voice told me to forgive her. I was certain I misunderstood what I was hearing, but the voice continued to chant those words, *"Forgive her, forgive her."*

All I knew was there was no way in hell I would ever forgive that horrible excuse for a human for all the damage she had done to me and I let it be known to whoever, whatever was telling me to do so. Why on earth would I forgive the person who tortured me my entire life? It just was not going to happen.

With that, the darkness wrapped itself around me once again, seemingly enveloping me. I felt my soul being led to a place even darker and deeper than before, pulling at my very being as if it were playing a game of tug a war as I tried to pull away.

Whatever had a hold on me suddenly let go, and I felt myself falling. I was frightened; I wanted so much to believe none of this was real; it couldn't be. I was hoping it was just a bad dream, a nightmare. But I knew deep within my soul what I was experiencing was indeed real, and there was no way to stop what was happening.

I spiraled down, faster and deeper, into what I am now sure were the bowels of hell. Once I realized where I was going, I begged to the God I now so wanted to believe in to save me. I begged him to stop this horrible journey into the ultimate depths of despair.

It was then I saw things, bad things, absolutely evil things. Creatures that have never seen the light of day, all howling, drooling. I am telling you, it was horrifying. They were everywhere, and so many of them. I could smell their decayed flesh and see their glowing red eyes, burning brightly in the darkness. I felt them as they moved around impatiently, watched me fall, with their mouths agape and tongues hanging out, like vultures, just waiting to devour me. I had never felt such dread and hopelessness. I was certain I was the next soul to be theirs for the taking.

I struggle even now to find the words to describe what I was experiencing, as I had never known such fear. I cannot put into words what I saw in those creatures; they were like nothing I had ever known before; so grotesque, so frightening.

The deeper I fell, the more it seemed to feed their howls, their cackling. It was almost as if they were laughing at what was to be my fate. I heard more sounds, different sounds, even more horrifying than those hideous creatures. What I heard could only have been the moans of souls in excruciating pain, the souls who had come before me. I was so afraid; the fear of what I experienced was incomprehensible.

I tried in vain to fight whatever was again tugging at me but had no power over it. I knew hell was my only destiny and I screamed in anguish, a scream that couldn't be heard as it blended with all the other tortured souls. Once again, I passed out.

When I gained awareness again, I found it odd. Things had become quiet; no voices, no creatures, nothing. I realized I had stopped falling and was once again in limbo.

It was then I heard a voice, a voice that seemed to be getting closer and closer, whisper, "You must forgive her."

I thought, *Oh my God, I am seriously going to hell if I don't forgive the person who made my life so unbearable? That's crazy!*

I knew I didn't deserve any of this. Whatever was causing me to experience this couldn't have been what everyone referred to as God. I told myself over and over if there were a loving God, none this would be happening; what kind of God would ever force you to do something you didn't want to do?

The voice continued chanting those words, "Forgive her." I heard two distinct voices speaking to me, then three. The number continued to grow until it sounded like a chorus of voices, oddly beautiful voices, repeating those words in a singsong way, rhythmically chanting, "Forgive her, forgive her," and as they did, the darkness began to lift once again.

I was taken aback when I realized I recognized one of the voices that was chanting. It wasn't long before I felt my mother there with me, encouraging me to forgive.

As the voices continued with their chanting, I felt my mother's presence, the gentleness of her touch; I heard my mother tell me how much she loved me, how she missed me so. She pled with me to let go of my anger, just to let it go, and promised me that once I did, I could be with her and my father in a new beautiful place. My mother told me how they had everything prepared for me; I just had to let go.

Then, like a train screeching to a halt, the chorus of voices stopped, and everything became eerily silent. It was then my mother spoke directly to me. "My child, you need to find it in your heart to forgive her now. Please, we have been waiting so long."

I lashed out at her, "But why? You tell me, why should I?"

I felt her presence pull away from me. My mother's voice coming from somewhere above me murmured, "Why not?"

Then she was gone. Once again, I was alone in the abyss with nothing but fear as my only company. I had never felt as lost as I did at that moment.

I became aware the darkness was lifting. It felt as if I were moving forward but could not be sure. The gradual lighting of black to gray was puzzling to me. I felt my non-body rise, then go down as if I were floating in the ocean. For the first time, I did not feel afraid. I know that sounds strange, but whatever was causing this to happen didn't seem evil. It wrapped me in what I can only call a loving embrace, gentle and comforting, and I no longer heard the cries of the damned. I was emotionally overwhelmed by the love that was emanating from whatever had just saved me. And then I blacked out.

When I came to, I realized I had returned to my sister's kitchen. I was confused, not able to comprehend how or why I was back there again but felt it was unjust.

Everything was just as it had been when I watched her earlier, but for one thing. I heard a sound that puzzled me. I looked around and found my sister and saw she was crying, actually crying. I couldn't help myself; I came closer to her, nearly touching her. I looked at her face and couldn't help but notice my sister was genuinely hurting; she was in despair. I continued to watch her for what seemed like hours as she rocked in her chair, her body shaking, her tears flowing, looking as if it would never end.

While it may sound horrible to say, I was glad to see her hurt. Never in a million years would I have thought my sister would do anything but rejoice at the thought of my passing. And to be honest, what I was witnessing before me was mesmerizing.

The next thing that happened was totally unexpected. I heard my sister cry out, "Oh dear God, I am so sorry for what I did to her, so sorry I hurt Terese. Now I have lost my baby sister! I never gave her a chance. Oh please, please forgive me."

My sister's chest heaved as she sobbed. I could almost feel her pain; I could see it was difficult for her. I, for the first time, wanted to wrap my arms around her to try and comfort her, but of course, I couldn't.

It was as if I were watching a movie in 3D with a plot change no one could have expected. I watched my sister as she pushed back her chair, put out her cigarette, and walked into the kitchen, her arms wrapped tightly around her as if she was trying to hold herself together. She went over to the phone on the wall and picked up the receiver, sobs still heaving in her chest. She looked at the caller ID next to the phone and dialed the number on it.

Her voice was shaky as my sister spoke into the phone. "This is Terese Manning's sister. I am sorry about how I reacted earlier. If it's okay, I would like to come down and take care of my sister now." She listened as she got a pen and paper to write down the address and told them she would be there shortly.

I couldn't believe what I was witnessing. My God, she, my horrible, awful sister, actually genuinely felt sorry for destroying my childhood, destroying me. My heart told me she was sincerely sorry and it opened up like a dam, the love I always wanted to feel for her pouring out of me. It was time; I had let go and forgiven.

It felt as if I were lighter than air as I moved close to her. I touched her gently on the shoulder and spoke those words I never imagined I would ever say to her. "It's all right. I love you. I forgive you."

My sister looked up in my direction as she put her hand on the shoulder I had just touched. At that moment, I believe she felt my presence and that she knew I was there with her.

At that, my sister broke down once again, seemingly speaking directly to me, "If only I could do it over again, I would do it differently. I would have loved you."

Hearing those words brought a sense of peace to me that I had never felt before. It freed me from the emotions I had for my sister. I finally realized just how much weight of the anger and resentment I had carried for my sister had held me down, aiding in turning me into a bitter, hard woman.

I felt the pain of my childhood lift from me – I basked in the joy of no longer carrying that burden on my soul.

I was so focused on her, I didn't notice things beginning to turn dark around me, fading into the blackness I had just escaped.

I continued to focus on her until there was nothing left to see. I hoped for her sake she would someday forgive herself and find the glorious peace I was just now experiencing, the peace she so desperately deserved.

Chapter Eight

I was astonished at the emotions that overcame me at that moment. I felt so good, so content with myself. By forgiving my sister, I was certain I had done all that was required of me to allow me to move forward, to join my mother, the only one I had ever felt loved by. I soon found out that wasn't to be.

Once again, I found myself falling back into the never-ending abyss of darkness. I had no idea why or how I got back there; I had forgiven, hadn't I? Wasn't this what it was all supposed to be about? Why was this happening again?

Instead, I headed right back to hell. Again, I heard the moaning and scream of those souls who were never going to be free, those souls trapped in the darkness with me. I lost that feeling of warmth in my heart as my soul plunged to hell. The sounds, so awful, continued to get louder and louder. I wondered how long they had been there and wondered even more if the blood-curdling sounds would ever end.

Seemingly out of nowhere, I felt a presence around me, enveloping me. Something evil had gotten so close, I felt it as it brushed up against me, almost as if guiding my soul into the never-ending blackness.

Startled, I tried to fight it, to get away from it, but soon realized any attempt was futile. It was as if evil itself were playing with me. Whatever it was, it continued to brush up against me, its touch stabbing the depths of my soul. It fed off my terror with each brush lasting longer and longer. Then I felt it. The evil had wrapped its tentacles around my very soul; I collapsed under the pressure of it. It was if it were trying to drain my soul of any possible hope. And if that was its plan, it was working.

I begged and pled to the entity to leave me alone, to let me go. But that wasn't going to happen. I heard a sick laughter, which sounded like wicked glee, and knew then leaving me alone was the last thing it wanted to do.

I felt myself spinning, spinning around at an incredible speed, disorienting me until once again, everything went black. Then I lost consciousness.

As I came to, I realized, with sudden clarity, that this must be the punishment for the way I had allowed hate and anger to have control over the life I had lived.

But wasn't living that life punishment enough? I had no joy, so little to love. Once my mother had died, the only brightness I had in my world was gone. I couldn't have changed who I was or how I felt; I had known no other way.

As the darkness continued to devour me, I thought maybe I did deserve what was happening to me. Why else would I continue to linger in that vast ugly darkness, surrounded only by pure evil, horror, and terror?

With each second, I felt howls and screeching of the damned closing in on me; pure evil continued to surround me, tearing my soul apart, bit by every painful bit.

The deafening sound of despair was all around me, growing louder in its horrid song. It should come as no surprise I could no longer comprehend what was happening to me. It wasn't until much later when I realized most of the gut-wrenching screaming I had heard was coming from me, as I fought to escape my personal hell. I felt fully insane, afraid of my own self.

I wasn't to be trapped inside my crazy mind for very long, though. Suddenly, I felt myself be lifted once again, by hands as gentle as silk, as comforting as a mother's love, calming my tortured soul and giving me false hope the nightmare was finally over. Again, I was wrong.

The next thing I knew, the darkness was gone and I was surrounded by the scent of stale flowers, when I realized those flowers were for me; I was at my funeral.

I was forced to be a silent witness of the last moments my body would be above the earth. It was hard to watch.

Chapter Nine

I must say I was a little hurt at the lack of turnout. There were maybe a handful of relatives who had come to show their respects, and surprisingly even a few of the people who were with me when I died, mostly out of curiosity, I am sure.

I looked over at my body and saw my sister standing at the head of my coffin, stroking my hair with one hand, blotting the tears that ran down her cheek with the Kleenex she held in her other hand. She stood like a sentinel, not leaving my side, barely responding to the few who came to give their condolences.

It was then I saw Joe, looking tired and so sorrowful, as he waited his turn to speak to my sister. When he got to her, he put his hand on her back. My sister turned toward him, bursting out into tears when she saw it was Joe.

Through her sobs, I heard her apologize to him, telling him it was because of her he never had a relationship with me. I learned my sister would go to Joe's coffee shop and tell Joe whatever he wanted to hear in the hope she'd get free donuts. On several of those visits, Joe shared his feelings for me with her. My sister assured him she would let me know, but never did. She said that if she had, maybe I would have been happy, maybe I would have still been there. She asked him to forgive her for denying me that happiness.

Joe held her with both arms as he seemed to take in the sight before him. It looked as if my sister, disheveled and puffy from crying, hadn't slept in days, seemingly so grief stricken by her loss.

It was clear to Joe that my sister was carrying much more guilt than simply not doing what Joe had asked. He knew there was something more to what he saw; it was if she had a much deeper pain eating away at her, something so dark he knew any words he might say would never bring comfort to her. Even so, Joe tried to console her.

He then reached out to my sister and pulled her into his arms to comfort her. That simple act of kindness only made her cry harder; feeding the stream of never-ending tears that flowed down her face.

I heard Joe try to comfort her as he told her not to cry; he said he forgave my sister for everything she had done to me. He pulled her away and looked into her eyes and said to her no matter what, nothing would ever change the fact that he had loved me.

Did he say he loved me? To say I was stunned by what I heard would be an understatement. I never knew he loved me. Oh my God, how had I been so blind? How could I not have known this? Why had I been so closed off in myself not to notice someone did care about me?

The answer to that question came almost as if on cue. The door to the funeral parlor opened and in walked Maximillian Heath, the man who made me the lonely, bitter woman I spent my adult life perfecting.

Seeing him as handsome as ever and dressed casually in jeans and a dark tee shirt, with his hair swept carefully over his beautiful dark eyes, I couldn't help but feel my heart beat faster.

Max was all I had ever wanted, seemingly so perfect in every way. In an instant, my weak moment of deeply buried affection for this man was swept aside as he walked with purpose directly to my sister as if he owned the moment. In disbelief, the feelings I experienced disappeared; the anger I had for him at his treatment of me began to overflow.

I knew this gorgeous excuse of a man, who now stood before my sister, was the very reason I never wanted to care about another person again. He sealed the fate of my desire to love when he had made me feel discarded like a worthless bit of clutter. No one would ever be allowed to get close enough to let that happen again.

Chapter Ten

It was because of that man, Max, that I refused to date as an adult. Because of him, I found caring about anyone only brought pain into my life. That I had even given him a chance was stupid. I had known if I opened myself up to anyone, no good could come of it; only heartbreak and devastation. I didn't realize just how devastated a person could get by rejection but found out quickly enough when I let my guard down and agreed to go out with him. After what he did, I vowed never to allow anyone else to hurt me like he did. Once was more than enough for me.

After his rejection, a handful of other boys made attempts to date me. My school had other outcasts just as unpopular as I who had built up the courage to ask me out, but I shut them down as quickly as the question came out of their mouths.

It may sound cruel to some, but the fact was, in a way, I enjoyed turning them down. It gave me a sense of power over the opposite sex that I had never had before or experienced since.

My teen years were tough enough, and I knew letting my guard down would only make things more difficult. I never stood out in school in any sense of the word. Rather, I was a part of the woodwork, as gray as the walls of the school I walked invisibly through each day, always hoping no one would notice me.

I went through each day, often without any real interaction at all. Maybe I was too hard on myself, but at the time, I had no love for myself; I felt ugly, so ugly I wanted no one to see me for fear of the taunting that was sure to come if they did. I was very petite – stick thin, actually – with big glasses that seemingly covered my entire acne-plagued face.

It wasn't just the way I looked that kept me quiet; there was my stammering whenever I spoke. I often struggled with my words whenever I did speak, only making matters worse.

By the time I got to high school, I didn't have any friends. All my friends from middle school treated me as if I were from another planet; so much so they would go out of their way to avoid me.

While it hurt, I told myself it didn't matter anyway. I had convinced myself those so-called friends had always been nothing but phony to me when we were younger, acting as if we were thick as thieves. I was sure then they were mocking me and made fun of me behind my back. I had to think that way; it made it easier for me to hate them a little more, each time they turned the other way when they saw me.

Because I was a loner, I usually had to be assigned study partners, because of the fact that no one was jumping up and saying, "Oh please, let me work with you! Please, just be my partner!" Instead, it was as if I had the plague. Whoever had been assigned to work with me never showed up to work on whatever our assignment was, leaving me to do all the work while earning them a greater grade for all my efforts. I despised every single one of those people for taking advantage of me.

On the second day of the second semester in my junior year, I was assigned to work on a science project with Max. I was beyond mortified at the thought of working with him. Because Max was everything I was not, I knew I was not going to be able to even look at him as we worked together on the project for fear of seeing him look down at me for being who I was. The only thought that ran through my mind was how dare the teacher to do this to me. What a cruel joke to put me with this boy.

Max was a year older than me, a senior who had the world in his hands. It was intimidating, to say the least, knowing how popular he was with everyone. Max played nearly every sport the school offered, and he played well. He was on the student council and seemingly a part of every other program there was offered at the school. Max excelled in them all. And unlike me, Max was invited to all the right parties and had all the right friends.

He was everything I was not, and I was sure he knew it.

I was surprised when I found out Max had asked to work with me on the spring science project. The teacher had someone else she had picked for me, but Max insisted, and no one ever said no to Max.

When I learned this, not only was I overwhelmed, I was also highly suspicious of his eagerness to have me as his partner. Why me when he could have any girl in the room or the school, for that matter? Every girl seemed to stop what she was doing just to stare at him whenever he came into the classroom. Maybe it was because Max was just all that, and though he never tried, he lived up to the cliché: tall, dark, and handsome.

Every time I looked at him, I couldn't help but notice his muscular arms, lean stomach, or the broadness of his chest. He was perfect in every way. And I loved how Max wore his jet-black hair parted on the side, framing his beautiful blue eyes.

He was the kind of guy fantasies were made of, what any girl in her right mind only dreamt of. With the perfect face, the perfect personality, it was obvious Max was what every girl wanted in a guy.

It was baffling how he stood there telling me he wanted me as his work partner. I couldn't help but brace myself for the humiliation I was confident he was setting me up for.

I would have done anything to get out of working with him but seemed frozen in place, trying to put words together to tell him I didn't think us working together would be a good idea. No words came out of my gaping mouth to protest. I watched as Max smiled at me with his beautiful smile and told me not to worry; he was sure we'd make a great team. What the hell did he know?

If I could have, I would have crawled under the closest desk and become invisible and never shown my face again. Don't think for even a moment I didn't feel the eyes of my classmates watching my every move, all the while laughing at my expense at the thought of Max wanting to me to be his partner. Mortified, I was certain

I heard the snickers and comments spoken under my classmates' breath.

There was no way I would work with him and said as much to my teacher. I asked her and then begged her to let me work alone, but she would have none of it. The teacher made it clear I had no choice; I would have to work with Max if I didn't want to fail the class. I felt my heart sink. It was the worst day of my life.

The first couple days we worked together, I didn't, couldn't, say a word, out of the fear I would start babbling nonsense and make a complete fool out of myself at my expense.

Max didn't seem to care I wasn't speaking to him. He, though, talked nonstop to me. He knew I was uncomfortable, so he told me I didn't need to speak at all if I didn't want to; Max assured me he could see my responses to what he had to say just by the look in my eyes. To make matters worse, Max said he liked how that looked.

I didn't believe him, not at all. I caught myself wondering how he could even see my eyes through my thick glasses. I was so embarrassed at what he had said, I looked away from him and wished he would just stop talking.

I held out hope Max would go away and find another partner. But he didn't. After a couple of weeks of working with him, I let my guard down a little. I began responding to his questions and found that I couldn't help myself as I listened in awe when he spoke.

It was then I realized I liked Max but knew how ridiculous that was because there was no way this guy would ever sink so low to like someone like me. I was nowhere near his league.

The last thing I wanted was for him to know I had feelings for him, so I did my best to hide my emotions but apparently didn't do a very good job. After working together with Max for three weeks, he turned my face in his hand toward his face as he smiled that smile that melted my heart and said, "You like me, don't you?"

I wanted to say, "Of course I do! Look at you! Who wouldn't like you?", but chose not to say anything and tried to pull my head away so my eyes didn't show him the truth. If he had known, I was certain that my feelings would chase him away. And there was that nagging thought that he was only asking just to get a reaction out of me.

On one of the last days we worked together, he asked if I were going to go to the football game that night. He said he was playing and would like it if I came to cheer him on. Cheer him on? What the hell did he mean, cheer him on? Why would he ask me to do that anyway? Was he just being nice or was he trying to set me up to be the butt of someone's joke? I wasn't about to give him that chance.

I told him I didn't like sports, so I wouldn't be going to cheer anyone on. He tried to persuade me to change my mind, but there was no way I was going to do so.

Once we finished up the project we were working on, life went back to normal; me, the non-existent girl and him, the high school sweetheart.

Well, not entirely back to normal. It seemed every time Max saw me in the school hallways, he would let me know he saw me, always with a little wave and the wink of an eye. I would look around to see if anyone else saw him showing me attention and if I didn't think anyone was looking, I would wave back and then quickly walk away.

On reflection, I don't know why I couldn't have been more receptive. After all, we worked together for an entire semester, so why should I feel like it was wrong every time Max looked at me? The only reason I can come up with is that I didn't believe the attention he was giving me was genuine.

Spring had arrived, and with it, the school bustled in preparation of the upcoming prom. The prom was something I tried not to acknowledge because I knew if I did, I would only be disappointing myself.

On a Friday night, about three weeks before the dance was to happen, I was home alone and had the house all to myself. Thankfully, my sister had gone out of town, and my mom had gone out to dinner, leaving me to fend for myself. Since I never could cook, I decided to order a pizza for dinner, then made myself comfortable on the couch and turned on the television.

About half an hour later, the doorbell rang and I thought it was the pizza delivery boy. I called out to him to wait a minute so I could get money to pay for the pizza.

It took me a few minutes to round up the cash I needed, but when I finally did, I went to the door and opened it. I was bewildered to see there was no delivery boy there; instead, in all his heavenly glory, Max was standing outside my door.

I was immediately self-conscious. Trying to wrap my brain around the situation, I wondered to myself how he would know where I lived. He had never asked, and I had never told him. I caught a glimpse of myself in the mirror next to the door and felt my stomach turn. I looked horrible. When I came home from school, I had thrown on an old paint-stained pair of sweat pants, along with one of my father's oversized, somewhat holey t-shirts to lounge on the couch in preparation for my Friday night television marathon. I had taken the braids out of my hair, setting my frizzy hair free. It was sticking out wildly about my head and I saw the makeup I had worn earlier was long gone. Never had I wanted to be seen looking like that by anyone, especially not Max.

I didn't have my glasses on, so for a fleeting moment, I hoped I was wrong. I squinted as hard as I could to see if it was Max; to both my shock and amazement, I knew it was him.

There Max stood, smiling that beautiful smile, with his adorable dimples seemingly piercing his cheeks as he looked at me.

I tried to comprehend his presence but just couldn't. It was like time stood still as we looked at one another. I was sure this was some set-up; guys like Max don't go to see girls like me. It was all I could do not to slam the door shut and hide in my room. I thought to myself,

What the hell is he doing here? I'm sure he saw the fear in my eyes.

Max ran his hand through his hair and smiled that much more. "Can I come in?" he asked. Was he kidding? I didn't know.

I stammered, "Max, why are you here?" He said he had something he wanted to talk to me about. What would he have to talk to me about? I didn't know of any school projects coming up that he would want to work with me on, so why would he want to talk to me of all people? What could be so important that he would come all the way to my house now?

Again, Max asked if he could come in. Since I didn't know what to say, I took a step back and let him in, still not knowing if that was the right thing to do.

I watched him as he stood in the front entry and casually looked around, seemingly taking in the view of my messy living room.

I couldn't help but think he was judging me; I was sure he was wondering how I could be such a slob. I turned from him to shut the door, hoping he wouldn't notice how uncomfortable I was. Once closed, I turned back in his direction, only to see him looking at me. Not staring like I was some circus freak; just gazing at me as if taking me in with those beautiful eyes. My palms began to sweat, and my stomach fluttered as if butterflies had just been released; it felt as if they were batting their wings in a mad attempt to escape. I thought I was going to throw up.

For what seemed like an eternity, we just stood there, just looking at each other. Out of an awkward silence, suddenly, as if an idea had just come to him, Max smiled at me and said, "I was just wondering if you were going to the prom this year."

I thought to myself, *What a stupid question for him to ask.* Of course I was not going! Why would I go? And really, why would he need to know if I were? Completely baffled at his question, I stammered, "No, I am not going." Not knowing what else to say, I blurted out, "Why? Are you going?"

Max made his way into the living room and sat down on the couch, locking eyes with me and said, "I don't know if I am. I haven't asked anyone yet."

The situation was getting stranger by the moment. "Oh, okay," I replied, and after another awkward silence, I asked, "Well then, why did you come here?"

Max patted the couch as if wanting me to sit next to him. Why on earth would he do that? Baffled by his presence, my mind scrambled as it tried to decipher what was happening.

Flustered, I sat down as far away from him as possible, on the chair across from the couch. All the while, I tried to make sense of this odd and completely unexpected visit. Again, I asked him why he came.

Max shook his head and grinned even more. "You are a little naïve, aren't you? I am here because of you."

Not any of this made sense to me. Max continued, "I came here to ask you to go with me to the prom. I want to take you. Would you go with me, please?"

My face flushed and I immediately felt anger rising within me. How dare Max come to my home and ask me out, knowing I was far beneath him? If it were a joke, it was a terrible one. How could he be so cruel? I knew, deep down in my heart, there was absolutely no reason for him to do so unless he had some ulterior motive.

Naïve, he said! Did he think I was stupid? I was far from stupid. Visions of that movie *Carrie* flashed through my head. I knew how this was going to play out; it would be just like it was for her. She was like me; she was a social outcast, a nobody. She fell for the guy who asked her out, only to be humiliated in front of the entire school. I certainly wasn't going to let anyone do that to me.

I jumped up from the chair, went to the door, and opened it. "Get out, now," I hissed at him. "This is not funny, and I don't appreciate you trying to make a fool out of me!"

Max stood up, all six foot two of him, with a confused look on his face. He asked with a voice that sounded so innocent, "Why? What did I do? What are you talking about?"

Barely containing myself, I told him, "This isn't funny. You know exactly what I am talking about. Leave now, or I will call the cops and say you broke in."

In a move I didn't expect, Max stepped closer to me to put his hand on my shoulder. I shrugged it away and told him once again to leave. When I looked at him, I saw he was no longer smiling; instead, he had a look more of hurt on his beautiful face.

For a brief moment, I thought maybe he was serious and did want me to go to the prom with him, but just as quickly, I corrected my thinking. I knew the truth; he didn't want to go out with me. He just wanted to make a fool of me.

Max shook his head as he went to the door and stepped outside. He turned to me and said, "You know you're wrong, don't you?" At that, I shut the door in his face. Heartbroken, I went up to my room and cried.

For what seemed like hours, the doorbell rang over and over, and I could hear him asking me to just open the door and talk to him. The pizza delivery boy came and went and still I wasn't going to open that door.

To think I had liked him, yet there he was, trying to set me up to look like a fool. I was sure he'd tell all his friends about how I freaked out and I knew I would be the laughing stock at school the next day.

Chapter Eleven

The next morning, I braced myself in anticipation of the humiliation I was certain I would face when I went inside the school. I was sure all the popular kids would be just waiting to point and laugh at me. But to my surprise, that didn't happen.

Halfway through the day, Max came up to me, not saying a word, and handed me a note. I took the note from him and walked away. I went to the bathroom and found an empty stall to read what he had written. I opened the note and saw his handwriting. He wrote, "Terese, I really do like you. Believe me, I am not kidding. Will you go to the prom with me?"

I put the note in my backpack and forced myself to go to class. That note, those words, kept playing on my mind. No matter how hard I tried, I couldn't focus the rest of the day.

The next morning, Max approached me again. This time, he asked, "Did you read the note?"

I told him I had, then asked him why he was doing this to me. He said he wasn't doing anything; Max said he just liked me and wanted to get to know me better. I didn't believe that for a moment.

My face flushed and my stomach did the butterfly thing again as I looked for a way to get away from him. The hallway was filling up as students were changing classes when I saw my chance and darted around him. Max tried to stop me, but I wouldn't let him. I heard him say he wanted my phone number so we could talk and as I practically ran away from him, I told him no.

Every day, there was another note, another plea for me to talk to him, to be his date. A week before the prom, I finally gave in and asked him, "Why me? Of all the girls you could choose from, why pick me?"

"Because you aren't like all the other girls," he replied. I thought to myself, well of course not! Look at me! Max continued, "You are real, and I like that about you. Would you please go to the prom with me?"

I thought about it for a few minutes as he stood patiently before me. I asked, "If I do, are you going to make a fool of me?" Max looked surprised by my words.

With what sounded like a bit of surprise and sincerity, he replied, "Of course not!"

For some reason, I let my guard down and I believed him. Something inside of me told me to stop fighting this, to enjoy someone like him, and accept someone like him wanted to go out with someone like me. I thought that maybe I wasn't so bad after all.

I told him I would and that he could pick me up at my house on prom night at around 7:00. I didn't tell him how I didn't want him to come earlier because my sister would still be home, because if he did, I knew she would do whatever she could to embarrass me. Max reached out and gave me a quick embrace. He said he'd be at my house at seven o'clock sharp but would call first to let me know he was on his way, if I would just give him my phone number.

I refused to give him my number. I knew if I did, it would only give my sister something else to taunt me about. Sensing my hesitation, Max knew not to push the issue any further, so just told me to be ready at 7:00 that night and he'd be there to get me, no matter what.

At that, I turned and walked away from him so he wouldn't see me beaming. For the first time in my life, I felt giddy. It was all too unreal! Here I was liked by the most popular boy in school, and I, plain little Terese, was going to prom with him. I couldn't wait to go home and tell my mother all about it.

As soon as I got home, I dropped my backpack and books on the floor next to the door and called out for my mother. She came into the living room to see me beaming. My mother was taken aback by my sudden happiness. She exclaimed, "Honey, it is so nice to see you smile! Tell me, what are you so happy about?"

My excitement poured out of me as I told her all about how I had met this boy who was super popular and how I had been asked to the prom by him. My mother seemed as happy as I and said, "Well, let's go shopping, then. You have a prom dress to buy!"

We shopped all afternoon, looking for just the right dress and just when I was about to give up, we finally found it. The midnight blue full-length strapless dress with an empire waist fit me perfectly; I was pleased with how it showed off the curvy figure I never knew I had.

I stepped out of the dressing room to show my mother how I looked. She openly beamed as I turned in circles, each time catching a glimpse of myself in the full-length mirror outside the fitting room door. I loved the feel of the material when it swished as I moved.

That day was without a doubt one of the happiest days of my life. Here I was, going to the prom with one of the most popular guys in school, and I would be wearing this beautiful dress! I thanked God for making this happen.

There was one little thing that would complete my new self-confidence, and that was not having to wear my glasses to the prom.

I had always wanted contacts. I asked for them in the past, but my mother always said no; it was her opinion that if you wore something on your eyes, you were risking your vision. I scoffed at the thought. I was already blind as a bat, and really, how much more damage could wearing contacts do to make my eyes any worse? Up until now, each time I asked, it was a losing battle.

This time was different, though. My mother was also swept up in the moment. She told me if contacts would make me happy, she would get them for me. I was more than pleasantly surprised; I was ecstatic. I went back to the dressing room to change and heard my mother say to someone, "Isn't she just beautiful?" I nearly cried in happiness when I heard her say that.

As soon as we got home, my mom got on the phone and made an eye appointment for me the very next day.

The way everything came together was amazing. I thought that maybe this was all just a dream. I had never felt this kind of happiness before or had ever seen my mother so pleased with me as she was now. I thought to myself, *If this is a dream, I hope it never ends*.

And you know the most amazing thing? Since I agreed to go with Max, I also looked forward to school. It was a thrill when Max made sure to sit with me at lunch. For the first time in my life, other kids began to warm up to me and acknowledge my presence. I felt like an entirely different person. It delighted me when Max would hold my hand as he walked me to class and amazed me when he would be waiting at the door to walk me home every afternoon. We had such amazing conversations about what we had learned at school that day. The best part of all was that Max didn't seem to care who saw us together, which only made me like him more. He made me feel special, made me feel like I mattered. I was his girlfriend and I loved every minute of his attention.

On the morning of the prom, I was so nervous when my mother and I went to the salon to get ready for the evening. My mother treated me to the works: a pedicure, manicure, and had my hair and makeup done.

The transformation was nothing short of amazing. Bit by bit, the stylist worked her magic and brought out the person I had always wanted to be. My nails sparkled from the mother-of-pearl polish, my hair went from a frizzy mess to an elegant up-do, securely fastened with a beautiful pearl barrette and what seemed like a can of hairspray. Then she brought out her palette of colors and went to work applying my makeup. I had never worn eyeliner or mascara or lipstick, fearing I would make myself look like a clown, but I put my trust in her hands. As she worked on me, the stylist told me how beautiful I looked and how lucky the boy was that was taking me out. I felt myself blush at such a compliment.

Once done, she turned my chair to face the mirror. I hardly recognized the beautiful girl who looked back at me. The stylist had performed absolute magic with her brushes and liners and lotions. Added with the benefit of wearing contacts and shedding my thick glasses, I finally felt worthy of going to the prom with the most handsome boy at school. I couldn't thank the stylist enough for her work. When my mother picked me up from the salon, she beamed at the sight of me, her little girl, who, for the first time in a very long time, was well groomed and grinning from ear to ear.

We returned home from the salon at around 4:30 and I immediately ran upstairs and got dressed. Since Max wasn't coming to get me for a few more hours, I had plenty of time to admire the new me. I was ecstatic with my new look and the promise of the evening. I counted down the minutes for Max to come to pick me up. I couldn't wait to see his face as I opened the door, displaying the new, beautiful version of me.

It seemed as if time moved at a snail's pace. When seven o'clock finally came, I was more than ready to go out on what really would be my first date. I just knew the night would be magical and, finally, my dark little life would change for good.

The magic of that night gave me hope that I would finally have a chance to live the life I had only dreamt of. And that was all because of Max. Being with him would finally allow me to be the popular girl I had always dreamt of being. I would have friends to share secrets with, to shop with; I would finally be alive!

But by 7:30, those dreams began to crash. Max hadn't shown up yet. A feeling of dread came over me, but I fought it, trying to reassure myself he must have had car trouble and was just running late.

I did my best to stay patient and positive as the minutes ticked on. When the clock struck nine o'clock, I had to accept the reality. I came to realize my hope, my dream of having a normal life, of having a boyfriend, were an illusion. It was all a horrible joke.

It was painfully clear Max never liked me at all. Now that I knew the truth, it became obvious he had played me. Surely Max and his friends had been laughing their asses off, amazed at how dumb I was to believe someone like Max would waste time on someone like me.

I was sickened by it all. How could I be so gullible to have believed him in the first place? I went to my room, took off my dress, and threw it on the floor, wanting to stomp on it, hating what it represented. I cried until I had no more tears to shed, all the while scolding myself for being so stupid as to fall for such a cruel joke. I questioned my judgment; why had I set myself up for such humiliation? I went over everything that led up to that moment and could not find a good answer for any of it. My mother tried her best to console me, but what good would that do? I refused her comfort. It only made me feel worse.

The following Monday, I refused to go to school. How could I? The humiliation and embarrassment were too much to handle. I was certain to be taunted and teased for being the loser I was. For nearly a week, I stayed in my room, not wanting anyone to talk to me. When my mother finally had enough of my pity party, she told me enough was enough. I was going back to school whether I wanted to or not.

As I forced myself out the door for school the next morning, my mother stood in the doorway and said to hold my head up high, act if nothing had happened, and go on with my life. I wanted to shout back at her, "Yeah, right, easy for you to say. You aren't the pathetic little loser who has to go back there and be made fun of."

I didn't, though. I knew any response I would have given would have fallen on deaf ears, so I did as I was told and returned to the last place I wanted to be. I went to school.

I entered the building with my head down, in an attempt to avoid any eye contact from anyone, for fear I would get teased, humiliated even more. I especially didn't want to lay my eyes on Max, who I was sure had a great laugh with his buddies when he told them how well he had humiliated me.

I made it to my locker with no incident and was just putting my backpack in it when I felt a hand on my shoulder. I froze when I heard Max say, "I am so sorry. Please, can you forgive me?"

Forgive him? How dare he? Hell would freeze over before I ever forgave that bastard. Max had tricked me, he took advantage of me, used me to be the butt of his joke. And now he had the nerve to ask me to forgive him? That was never going to happen.

I turned to him, my eyes as cold as ice, and spat, "Do not ever talk to me again, don't even look at me. You are the worst person I have ever met and I truly, honestly hate you." With that, I slammed my locker door shut and stormed away, leaving him standing there, speechless.

Max tried time and again to talk to me, to apologize, but I wasn't about to listen to anything he had to say. He eventually gave up trying, but every time I saw him, he'd look at me with a sadness in his eyes that should have made me want to reach out to him, but it didn't; it only made the contempt I had for him grow stronger.

I vowed never to let my guard down again; to never trust another human being, because I knew, and Max had proven it, anyone who tried to gain my trust was nothing but a fox in sheep's clothing. I wasn't about to let another fox thrive on my pain; one time was one too many.

Now, thirteen years later, there he was, my first love, the love who destroyed me, at my funeral, standing next to my sister as he looked at my dead body, tears rolling down his face.

My sister asked him who he was and he told her he was the boy who was supposed to take me to the prom. My sister was clearly surprised he had shown up at my funeral, and asked him how he could hurt me so. I was devastated by his response.

Max replied softly, "I swear, I never wanted to hurt your sister."

My sister visibly flinched, the cold in her words undeniable.

"Is that right? Well, it's a little too late for that. Because, Max, you did hurt her; you hurt her bad. Did you know she never got over you or what you did to her?"

"It just couldn't be helped. Honestly. On the day of the prom, my appendix burst and I ended up in the hospital; I wasn't able to do anything about it." Max choked the words out. "I-I never planned not to show up. Why would I?"

It looked as if my sister wasn't sure of what Max was telling her, "What are you talking about?"

"Oh my God, I liked your sister! It took forever just to get her to go with me as it was. Please believe me, I never meant for anything bad to happen."

As tears freely flowed down my sister's face, she responded, "Oh my God, Max, I wish I had known that. You have no idea how much I threw how you dumped her in her face. I made her feel even worse. What was I thinking? How could I have been such a bitch to her?"

It seemed as if Max didn't hear her words. He seemed lost in the pain he had felt for disappointing me, then continued as if talking to himself, "Your sister never forgave me. I tried talking to her, but she wouldn't listen."

My sister looked at him, not knowing what more to say. Her eyes glistened with tears as she took in his words.

Max, his voice breaking, said, "I would have had my parents call her that night to let her know what had happened but couldn't. I had no way of reaching her. For some reason, Terese refused to give me her phone number."

"That was because of me." My sister turned from Max to my body and leaned in close, begging my dead body to forgive her for what she had done. Her words moved me.

She touched Max gently on his arm and confessed, "It was my fault. I am so very sorry. Please forgive me."

Again, it was as if Max didn't hear her. He continued, "The day I went back to school after recovering from the surgery, I saw her at her locker, and I tried to talk to her. I tried to explain what had happened, but she didn't want to hear any of what I had to say. I won't ever forget the look in her eyes. She looked at me with pure hate; it was horrible."

My sister, lost in her misery, gave him a hug and told him she understood. She said she was certain if I had given him a chance to explain himself, I would have understood as well.

Max turned back to my casket and gently touched my hands, my face. He spoke to my body so quietly, I strained to hear his words. Now I wish I hadn't because I hated myself for what he said next.

Max asked me to forgive him. He stroked my hair and whispered to my dead body how he wanted to take me to the dance, that he was sorry he couldn't and said he how he wished I would not have been so stubborn; he told my cold body how he wished I would have listened to him when he tried to explain that day at my locker. Max closed his eyes and kissed my forehead, my eyes, my cheeks, and finally my lips, ever so gently, then turned to my sister and said, "I never had a chance with her. I wish I had. I never got to tell her I loved her. I loved her so much." At that, my sister broke down completely. A relative led her out of the room.

He loved me? I couldn't believe what I had heard. Now two men had come to my sister and told her how they felt. Both good, caring men had loved me and, in my insecurity, I was too blind to realize it. My soul filled with heaviness so thick and a feeling of loss so heavy over what could have been.

And it was no one's fault but my own. I cursed myself for my life. Because of my stubbornness, my anger, my self-centeredness, so deeply ingrained in my soul, I had no idea of who I had been, and because of that, how I hurt the very people who cared the most about me. I had been certain anyone who was kind to me was only out to hurt me. How could I have been so blind? How could they ever forgive me? How could God ever forgive me for the monster I was?

My spirit moved as close to Max as possible in the hope he would feel my presence, and I whispered to him, "I hurt you, and I am sorry. I pray you can forgive me for being such a horrible human being. "

Max seemed lost in his grief. I just wanted to hold him, comfort him, but it was far too late for that. I could do nothing but bear witness to the pain I caused.

I felt my heart break over all over again, and this time, it was because of me, of what a fool I had been. Moving as close as I could to Max and hoping beyond hope he would hear me somehow, I whispered in Max's ear, "I was so afraid of being hurt that I hurt you. I am so sorry, my love; please forgive me. I want you to know I loved you too."

My soul ached with a mixture of sorrow, desire, and even love. How I wanted to wrap my arms around him and hold him close, so close to me.

But of course, it was too late to anything in the physical sense. The best I could do was to hope Max knew I had forgiven him for thinking he would purposely hurt me. I told him how ashamed and heartbroken I was over building a wall no one, not even Max, could tear down. In my stubborn ignorance, I believed I had been protecting myself from the pain of love.

I prayed he could forgive me for what I had done to him and prayed even harder Max would find the love he so richly deserved.

I am sure he had sensed my presence when I saw him shiver a little, as if a chill went up his spine. Max looked around to see if anyone else heard or felt what he had experienced. Of course, no one could have heard anything. Those words were for him alone; no one else could have heard me.

Confused by what he had just experienced, he seemed to question his sanity a little. Max thought that maybe he'd just heard a ghost speak to him but dismissed the thought immediately, realizing how silly it would sound if he said anything, so he said nothing and prepared to leave the funeral home. He said goodbye to my sister and left the funeral home as his heart felt a little less burdened.

Max was such a good man. I wished I could go back and make things right between us but knew it was too late. I would never forgive myself for being so hard on him. My life would have been so different if only I had listened to what Max tried to tell me that day.

All of the loathing and bitterness I felt for others turned itself onto me. I desperately wanted to leave this place, this funeral, this honoring of my pathetic life. I could no longer stand looking at the monster I had become.

I now welcomed the blackness and prayed it would take me away from here, take me to where my dark soul belonged. But no matter how much I wanted to leave, I couldn't. Leaving was not in the cards just yet. I wasn't able to stop what was playing out before me and, knowing that, I felt like I was dying all over again.

Chapter Twelve

Moments before the visitation was over, I noticed a slim, honey-blonde-haired woman dressed professionally in a black, knee-length business suit, standing inside the entrance of the funeral home, tentatively looking around the room as if she were unsure she was in the right place. Dark sunglasses covered her eyes and her face was nearly covered by a handkerchief she held.

The strange woman stood there for a long time, taking in the room and the people mingling about. I struggled to understand who she was and why she was there. It was then that I noticed the ring on her finger and it came to me. This was the woman who had pretended to be my friend, the person who I shared my deepest dreams and secrets with. And this was also the woman who fired me from my dream job. *Of all people to show up*, I thought incredulously, *What in the hell is she doing there?*

I wanted her to leave, to turn around and go back out the door she came in through, but she didn't. Instead, she walked up to my sister, who had once again taken her place at the head of my casket, and extended her hand.

"I worked with your sister a few years back," she volunteered to my sister. "I was so sorry to hear she had passed on; I want to give you my condolences. Your sister meant the world to me."

Unbelievable! The nerve of her, of all people, to show up at my funeral! The sorrow I had felt for my treatment of Max dissipated as rage filled my soul. How dare she show up and act as if she cared! This woman took everything I had ever worked for away from me.

She was a snake, a deceiver. The entire time we worked together, she acted as if she liked me. She pretended to be my friend, until the day I came to work and she fired me, totally blindsiding me. In a shrill voice, she ordered me to pack up my stuff and leave immediately.

Dumbfounded, I did as she ordered and packed fourteen years of my life in three boxes provided by the janitor, then left the building. I was at a loss as to what I would do next. This woman had no qualms at turning my world upside down. Her presence at my funeral made me so angry, so appalled. How dare she have the nerve to stand there and give her phony condolences.

I Died Yesterday

If I could have willed myself back into my body, I would have done it just to get her to leave my funeral in the same manner she made me depart the job I worked my entire career for. Abruptly.

But of course, I couldn't do anything but hover above her and shoot her some of the most evil looks she would never see.

I moved as close to her as possible, causing her to shiver. I relished the thought I was able to reach her even though she had no idea it was me that gave her chills. How I wish she had known.

It was nothing less than horrible to be forced to watch and listen to her as she cried her big crocodile tears, sniffling and blowing her nose in the very same lace handkerchief I had given to her to celebrate her promotion at work.

This woman was Karen, the woman who had so deftly pretended to be my friend. What a hypocrite she was. The very sight of her filled my soul with disgust.

Her display of mourning was unforgivable; downright disgusting, actually. I couldn't believe the gall of Karen standing there, in front of my dead body.

She turned from my sister and stood before my casket; I watched her as she knelt down, crossed herself, and began to pray. She reached out and stroked my cold, dead hand. The nerve of her! She acted like she was the friend I once believed she had been.

Karen and I had met in school, and we hit it off. We had landed our dream jobs in a prestigious law firm after graduating from college as paralegals. We started working at the firm on the same day and would laugh about how we were the lowest on the totem pole, and that was great because if we thought that way, we figured we wouldn't get hurt.

I was not a person with friends, but Karen became an exception. She could make me laugh at the drop of a hat. I had secretly wished she were my sister, instead of the one I had who tormented me any chance she had.

I stood by her side when she met her future husband. I had even been the maid of honor in Karen's wedding. I held her hand when she gave birth to all three of her children. But things changed when she got her promotion at work. She began wearing sunglasses at work. She would come in later and later, sometimes smelling of alcohol. When I tried talking to her about it, she became distant. After a time, she didn't speak to me at all anymore. That hurt. It should have woken me up, made me realize she was nothing to me. But it didn't. And then she fired me.

Karen extended her hand to my sister. "I know you don't know me, but Terese was my best friend," she told my sister. Karen knew my relationship with my sister and knew I hadn't talked to her in years, so how could she assume my sister would know her? Karen went on, "We had a parting of the ways, and I feel horrible about it."

"What happened?" my sister inquired.

"I didn't have the heart to tell her my situation at home and work. My husband is abusive."

All I could think was, *That is a bunch of bull.* Whenever I was with the two of them, all Karen's husband ever did was cater to her every whim. The shock I felt when Karen then took off her sunglasses, exposing a black eye along with some bruising on her cheek, took my breath away.

Karen continued, "I became my husband's punching bag, and I knew how much Terese liked him, so I didn't tell her."

Oh my God! I had no idea. I was her best friend. Why wouldn't she tell me? I would have helped her. I would have been there.

"After my promotion, my husband quit his job and went on a spending spree. He put us in massive debt, and I was the only one paying the bills. On the day I let your sister go, something I never wanted to do, I was called into my boss's office. He told me I had to let three people go or I would lose my job. I couldn't afford to lose the job, with three kids and a husband who would kill me if I had. My boss told me the three people he wanted to let go, and when I heard Terese's name, I begged him not to fire her. I told him how important she was to the firm. But he wouldn't hear anything I said. He told me I had to let her go or I was done working with the company. Our boss had me backed into a corner. I did what I was forced to do. I let Terese go. It was the worst thing I have ever done. She never spoke to me again. I tried calling her, even went to her house, but she wouldn't answer the phone. She wouldn't answer the door. I lost my best friend that day."

My sister said, "I am sure if she would have listened, she would have helped you. She would have understood."

"I felt horrible about it, still do. I found a job for Terese at a competing firm but was not able to reach Terese to let her know. Had she taken it, she would have been a top administrator. I wish things had turned out differently."

My God. What kind of friend was I that I didn't see the signs? My friend was struggling. My friend was hurting. She never wanted to hurt me; she loved me. She loved me. And I hated her for it. Dear God, what is wrong with me?

I moved close to Karen, and though I knew she wouldn't hear me, I told her I forgave her and asked her to forgive me. Karen shivered a little, leaned over my casket, and kissed my cheek. With tears running down her cheeks, she said, "I will always love you, Terese, and I want you to know, you will always be my best friend." Everything went dark.

Chapter Thirteen

I was back in the limbo that seemed to hold me in its grip. The darkness seemed a little softer, a little more comfortable. My heart seemed to be less hardened. I clearly had misjudged so many people, and I let it rule the way I lived. I felt nothing but loathing of myself. How, I asked myself, could anyone like someone was cruel and judgmental as I?

It seemed as if things changed quickly this time. I went from blackness so deep and dark it made my skin crawl, to a smoky gray to daylight, where I was in a room that clearly belonged to a small boy.

I took in the room, mystified as to where I was and why. I noticed there were posters on every wall, with vintage baseball stars from various major league teams: Babe Ruth, Jackie Robinson, and Hank Aaron were prominently featured.

As I continued to take in what I was seeing, I noticed the posters were in pristine condition, which was odd to me. I thought I had gone back in time or the child's parents were unabashedly obsessed with the 1950s in their décor of this child's room.

I continued to inspect the room. In the corner sat a rocking horse, which looked vaguely familiar, and on the floor next to it was a discarded cowboy hat, lying upside down as if it had been thrown off while the child who occupied this room was riding his bucking bronco.

The bed was a small twin size bed, neatly made, the corners tucked in military style. On top of the bed was a child-sized robe, and across the bottom of the bed lay a crumpled child-sized blanket embellished with Roy Rogers. By the size of the bed and the robe, I deducted the child who occupied this room was a boy who must have been around the age of five or six years old.

Scanning the room, I noticed the abundance of toys scattered all about the room and I caught myself getting a bit angry. It was obvious to me the child who slept and played here was spoiled. Compared to this room, the room I had grown up in and had shared with my sister may as well have been a prison cell.

Why on earth would I be in the room of a spoiled brat? And why, for God's sake, would I be in a room that seemed to have existed a good thirty years before I was even born?

I would soon find out when, suddenly, the room burst to life. A dark-haired little spitfire of a boy threw the door open and ran with purpose to his overly stuffed toy box. Lifting the lid, he put his little head in and began tossing toys over his shoulder until he had a pile of toy trains, play six shooters, gun holsters, and a pair of cowboy boots lying behind him.

"No, not this," the boy said as he chucked train car after train car. "Not that," he said to the pop gun. "Oh, I know you are there; it's time for war! Come on, where did Mommy put you?"

After seemingly emptying out the bottomless toy box, he clapped his hands in delight and smiled. "There you are!" The boy pulled out a plastic bag that held his precious prize. The bag was filled to its brim with little green plastic army men and an array of tanks and weaponry.

In his high little boy voice, the boy chanted, "The Russians are coming! The Russians are coming! We need to fight them, men!" With that, he unceremoniously dumped the bag out and spread his little green troops all over the floor. He immediately began separating his forces, so engrossed in his mission, he failed to hear the voice coming somewhere from below.

"Hey, sonny boy, you need to wash up now. It's time for dinner!" It was a woman's voice – apparently his mother – soft and almost singsong. The boy, too busy to notice, continued playing.

I watched silently, thinking of how nice it would have been if I had been called to dinner like that.

Instead, I was told to get my ass to the table and to hurry, or I'd "get mine." Dinner was always five o'clock sharp, and if you weren't at the table on time, you knew you were going to bed hungry. And that was only after the lecture of how hard Daddy had to work for the food he put on the table and how it was disrespectful to both him and my mother if I couldn't show my appreciation for what he provided or my mothers' cooking. Considering my poor mom was a horrible cook, it seemed to get to the table on time to eat what she created in the kitchen made being sent to bed hungry nothing more than a small inconvenience.

The little boy disregarded his call to dinner and continued with his imaginary war with himself. I stepped closer to him, trying to understand why I was here. What could a little boy have to do with my journey? None of this made any sense.

The little boy looked up and spoke directly to me. "Who are you?"

There was just him and me in the room, and he surely couldn't see me! But I looked at him, and sure enough, he was staring right at me! He repeated, "Who are you?"

I froze. It was clear this little boy could see me. My God, what was I going to do now? How could I explain this to a mother who would want to know what I was doing in her son's room? I had no explanation.

I looked for a place to hide and darted behind the curtains.

His bedroom door flew open, and the boy ran to his mother's arms. His mother was the perfect 1950s wife. She wore her dark auburn hair neatly tucked into a bun, and wore a light blue plaid housedress with a flowered apron covering most of it. The only thing missing were the pearl necklace and high heel shoes.

If she had been wearing that, I would have sworn I stepped into a 1950s sitcom. Her delicate beauty struck me. She had vibrant green eyes, high cheekbones, and a perfect nose. For some reason, I was sure I had seen her somewhere before. I knew this woman, but how?

"Honey, what's wrong?"

Pointing directly to me as I tried in vain to hide behind the curtains, the boy told her, "Mommy, that lady is in my room!" If she saw me, I knew for certain I was going to have a problem. I scrambled to try to find an excuse to explain how I came to be in the boy's room.

"What lady?" she asked her son.

"That one, right there!" the boy insisted as his finger continued to point at me. I was dumbfounded. My mind was scrambling, trying to find a logical explanation for what was happening. There was none. His mother looked in the direction he was pointing. Oh, my God, I am dead, aren't I? Why can this kid see me?

His mother shook her head and replied, "Oh, honey, don't be silly. There isn't anyone there."

"But, Mama, there is! She is right there! Go look."

His mother walked over to the curtain, pulled it open, and totally exposed me. "You silly boy, I love you and your imagination, but there is no one there! Now that's enough, son. Enough play. It's nearly five o'clock. Dinner is ready. Let's wash your hands now. Your daddy is waiting for us."

The little boy insisted, "But, Mommy, that lady is looking right at you!"

His mother looked in my direction once again, pretending to see me, and said, "Oh, now I see her. That must be your guardian angel." She spoke as if trying to humor her son,

"Hello, Angel, Tommy has to have dinner now. Thank you for keeping him company, but we are going to eat now." With that, she walked out of the room, the little boy staring at me as he followed her out the door.

I heard them go into the bathroom and turn on the water in the sink. I looked around the room again and realized then where I was.

I thought about the story my father had told me about his childhood that never left him and said it had always brought him comfort during his hardest times. He talked about a woman being in his room that only he could see. My father saw her time and again, most often when he was at war. He told me she was a beautiful vision; she was his personal guardian angel. My father shared with me how he felt oddly calm and comforted whenever she came around.

My father said his angel stopped coming around when I was born, and he believed it was because of me that he never saw her again. That was hard for a little girl to hear from a man she had wanted love from. My father had been a big believer in spirits and ghosts and such. We all thought he was a crackpot and we would tease him, telling him the woman was everywhere, that we could see her too. But of course, we couldn't. Now I knew why.

My father was telling the truth. Now, standing in this room, surrounded by little boy paraphernalia, I realized my father had known me before I was born. That little boy was my very own father, and he had seen me long before I ever existed and he thought I was his guardian angel.

None of this made any sense. A chill went down my bodiless spine. Why on earth would I be here? What did any of this have to do with me? What was the purpose of seeing my father as a little boy? I was confused, but as moments passed, I found myself growing resentful. How could such a loved child grow up to be a hateful man? Here he had every privilege in the world, as evidenced by the overabundance of toys scattered all about his room, yet he willfully denied his daughters the same experience. My father would rant on about how toys "made you soft," how they made you imagine a way of life that wasn't real, and that he wasn't going to raise his kids to become disillusioned like he was when he went out into the world. Playing was for the weak. Work built character. So, instead of allowing us to play, he worked us like dogs. He said we would thank him in the end. Oh, how wrong he was.

My disgust wasn't as strong as my curiosity, and I found myself moving to the bathroom door, keeping myself out of the line of vision so I wouldn't be seen again.

At my vantage point, I watched the woman, my grandmother, carefully washing my father's hands. Was my father so coddled he couldn't even wash his own hands, for crying out loud?

The sight repulsed me. I screamed out in my voiceless way, "Stop it! Let him wash his dirty little hands, for God's sake!"

Once my grandmother finished washing my fathers' hands, she knelt down and dried the boy's hands. She spoiled him to the point of ridiculousness. Then she looked him in the eyes and said, "Sonny boy, do you know how much I love you?"

My father outstretched his arms as far as he could and said, "This much?"

My grandmother pulled him to her and exclaimed, "Oh yes, that much and so much more!"

My father buried his face in her hair and said, "I love you that much too!" With that, she picked him up, and they went down the stairs to have dinner.

I didn't follow them immediately. Instead, I stood on the landing at the top of the stairs, trying to comprehend what I had just witnessed. My father was such a loving little boy. He had experienced love, and he gave it back freely. He was a happy little child. What on earth caused him to change? For some reason, my heart broke. I felt what seemed to be tears stream down my face. What happened to that little boy that could change him so drastically? Honestly, I was confused by my feelings. Was I crying for him or were the tears that wouldn't stop for me? Was it that knowing this happy, loved little boy would one day grow up to be a tyrant to his children? What could have happened to this little boy to drastically change him into the monster he became? Little did I know I would soon find out,

Chapter Fourteen

I made my way to the familiar dining room, a room I spent a lot of time in when I was a child. We would go to dinner every Sunday, but it wasn't a happy event. I don't recall even one Sunday dinner that didn't end in a vicious argument between my father and my grandfather.

The mood in the room was light and relaxed. A dog, a golden lab, meandered into the room and went right to my father's chair and lay down next to it. My father reached down and patted the dog on the head and beamed at his mother, knowing if he smiled big, she wouldn't have the heart to tell him to let the dog out while they ate.

My grandfather, a handsome man, sat at the head of the table. It touched me as I watched my father pull his chair close to my grandfather on the right side of the table, my grandmother at the other end of the table.

My mouth, if I had one, would have been watering in anticipation of eating the spread on the table of delicious food just waiting to be eaten. My grandmother was an excellent cook, and she loved nothing more than making a tantalizing meal that you couldn't wait to devour.

"Hey there, son, come here and give your old dad a hug!" My father jumped out of his chair and fell into his father's arms, giving his dad the biggest hug he could.

My grandfather looked at his son and beamed with love in his eyes. "Oh my goodness, you are getting so strong! You are growing into such a little man!"

My dad pulled up his shirtsleeve and flexed his little arm, trying to work up a muscle. "Daddy, see how strong I am?"

My grandfather grinned as he felt his little boy's bicep and said, "You are the strongest boy in the whole world! I am so proud of you, little man!"

"Daddy, I am going to start playing baseball tomorrow! I am so excited to play ball! Do you think I will be as good as Hank Aaron?"

"I am excited too, my son! You will be better than Hank Aaron, of that I am sure. And guess what? I am going to be your coach. How do you like that?"

"That is so great, Daddy! Can we play catch after dinner?"

Ruffling his son's hair, he responded, "Of course, son, just as soon as we eat!" With a gleam in his eye, my grandfather added, "And don't feed the dog. You clear your plate on your own, young man!"

"I will, I promise! I love you, Daddy!" My father got down on his father's lap and took his place at the table. My grandfather looked at his little family contentedly and then led them in prayer. Once done, I watched this happy family begin to eat, to laugh, and to talk about their day.

I was truly baffled. I had never seen my grandfather show any affection whatsoever to my father. I had never seen my grandfather pray. It was as if I were in a bizarre episode of the *Twilight Zone*. Honestly, I would have never imagined my father's childhood to be so perfect. But then, my dad never spoke of his childhood.

Chapter Fifteen

At that moment, before my eyes, the room seemed to shift somehow and change. I was still in my grandparents' dining room, but things weren't the same. The little boy who'd been sitting at the table with his dog lying at his feet was now a young man. The dog that had been at my father's feet was no longer there.

I noticed a picture on the dining room wall that hadn't been there before. It was a family picture with my father, grandfather, grandmother, and a beautiful, curly-headed golden-haired, little girl who appeared to be around the age of three. I didn't understand. Who was this child? I never heard of my father having a sibling. It was all very strange.

My brain struggled to understand this change, and I found myself looking around for answers. I looked closer at my grandparents, and though I knew it was them, it seemed they looked a little different, years older somehow.

The silence in the room was a sharp contrast from the laughter that filled it only a moment ago. My grandmother's eyes, which had twinkled with delight only moments ago, were now puffy and red as if she had just been crying. My grandmother's hair, usually coiffed to perfection, was haphazardly swept up in a bun and sprinkled with strands of gray; her frame looked smaller and somewhat frail, nearly lost in the button-down sweater she had wrapped around her. I wanted to hug her, to bring back the loveliness that was now missing from her beautiful face.

As I looked over to my grandfather, I noticed his face had changed as well. His usually smiling face was now solemn and somehow hardened. My grandfather's eyes were hidden behind dark horn-rimmed glasses that I had never seen before.

Time had certainly passed somehow, some way, and no matter how big his glasses were, the small but noticeable creases and wrinkles around his eyes seemed to be enhanced by those rims.

The joy in the room was gone. Instead, sadness prevailed, and the silence in that room was so pronounced, it was palpable.

My eyes were drawn to my father. He was at least ten years older than he had been just a moment ago, and had grown from a sweet little boy into a handsome, sullen-looking young man of maybe sixteen years of age. My father wore a baseball uniform and had on a baseball cap, with beautiful dark curls peeking out from underneath. He was no longer that smiling little boy; instead, he looked as if he had the weight of the world resting on his shoulders.

It was obvious my father was uncomfortable. He kept his head down as he pushed the food on his plate around, not eating anything. He didn't make eye contact with either of his parents. I sensed something was very wrong and, when I looked at my father; he looked as if he were a million miles away, lost in his private thoughts.

The ominous silence was broken when my grandmother spoke in a near whisper, "Do you have to go to your game tonight, son?"

Without looking up, my father quietly responded, "Yes, Mom, I do. I am the only pitcher the team has. They need me."

My grandfather looked to my father, his eyes cold, and sternly said, "Too bad for them. We just buried your sister. We need you here."

That once happy boy who had such a contagious smile looked at his father with tears glistening in his eyes. In one swift move, my father pushed his plate away from him and stood up. "My being here isn't going to bring her back, Dad. I am going!"

With that, my father got up, turned his back on his parents, and stormed out the front door. My grandfather, angry at his son, stood up, went to the door, and angrily shouted, "If you leave now, don't ever come back! You killed your sister! We don't need you. You are a coward."

My grandmother sat paralyzed as she watched my grandfather; she begged him to stop. But my grandfather kept up his rampage, telling my father he was nothing, he'd never be a man, he would never be anything.

My father jumped into his car and never looked back. My grandparents looked at one another as tears rolled my grandmother's cheeks.

My father left home the day the funeral was held and never came back. He moved in with his girlfriend, my mother's family. My mother was the only one who could make him smile; make him feel like he was worth something. She knew how he suffered for having run over his sister.

Chapter Sixteen

The day his little sister died was burned into his memory, into his soul. He never forgave himself for what happened that day.

My dad had just gotten his driver's license and was excited to drive himself to his baseball game for the first time. He had jumped in the car and put the car in reverse. He looked out his car window and saw his little sister riding her tricycle down the sidewalk in front of the house. He looked away from her, adjusted his mirrors, then began to back down the driveway. He never saw his little sister ride her tricycle down the sidewalk and behind the car; it had happened in an instant. As he stepped on the gas, he heard a sickening thud and immediately knew he backed into something. He put the car into park, jumped out, and went to the back of the car. There lay his little sister. My father fell to his knees, calling out her name. "Margie, Margie, wake up! Oh my God! Wake up!"

My grandmother heard my father's cries and ran out the door to her son to find her young daughter lying unresponsive under the car. She called out to my grandfather, "Call an ambulance. Margie is hurt."

"Mom, it was an accident! I didn't mean to hurt her." Pointing to the sidewalk, my father continued, "Margie was standing right there. I saw her on the sidewalk. I never saw her go behind me. I am so sorry, Mom; please forgive me!"

My grandmother comforted her son. "It will be all right. Margie will be all right."

My grandfather came out and saw his son in distress, his baby girl lying motionless. "What the hell? What happened? What did you do?" he yelled at his son.

"I didn't know, Dad!" my father pleaded with his father. "It was an accident! I didn't know Margie was behind me!"

"You killed your sister! What the hell is wrong with you?"

"I didn't see her; I swear I didn't. Oh my God! Dad, oh my God! I am so sorry, I didn't know Margie was behind the car," my father cried out. "I am so sorry! I didn't see her there."

My grandfather went over to his lifeless daughter and held her in his arms. He looked up at his son with disgust and hatred in his eyes. "It's a little late for sorry, don't you think? Your sister is dead because you killed her. Damn you. Go to hell!"

My father, in his devastation, went to his room and in desperation and sorrow, contemplating taking his life. My grandmother came to him and comforted him. She told him everything would be fine, that she understood. But nothing was fine after that. It was never fine after that.

Chapter Seventeen

In 1964, my father was drafted into the Army. Before being sent to boot camp, he proposed to my mother and promised her a life filled with love and joy upon his return. While at boot camp, he wrote to my mother every day, expressing his undying love to her. In one letter, he asked her to plan a wedding for them upon his return from boot camp. And so she did. The day after he came home, he married my mom, the love of his life.

My father was so handsome that day, dressed in his uniform; my mother truly was a vision in a simple white wedding gown, with a veil that only enhanced her natural beauty. They were married in her parents' backyard, surrounded by flowers from my grandmother's bountiful garden, with family and friends witnessing their day.

His mother, my grandmother, beamed with pride, dabbing at her eyes as they said their vows to one another. It was perfect, but for one thing – the absence of my grandfather. My father had hoped my grandfather would attend this very special day in his life. He wanted nothing more than to have the love of his father, the blessing of his father. My father longed for his forgiveness. What would have been a perfect day was spoiled by the fact that his father was not there for him. My father had hoped his father would be there, be proud of his son. But that was not to be.

Chapter Eighteen

It was as if I were watching a movie, but not just any movie; this was the story of my father's life. Why in the world would I see this? Time moved forward, and I was there when my father was deployed to Laos in 1964, as he left my mother newly pregnant with my sister; I watched as his world was turned upside down.

Leaving my mother was the most difficult thing he had ever done. The tears flowed down his face as he boarded the plane that would take him to a foreign land, to a war he was not prepared for. My father didn't want to take part in a war he didn't believe in. He didn't want to take the life of another. But he had no choice. He had to go.

By 1964, the North Vietnamese Army and the Viet Cong had successfully expanded their operations in Laos and South Vietnam. The cost to the U.S. military in manpower had reached 225 troops' deaths.

I witnessed my father cry every night as he flinched every time he heard a bullet. I saw him suffer and change as his heart began to harden every time one of his brothers in his platoon was wounded or was killed by those he began to recognize as his enemy. Within his first three months, he had lost eight of his fellow troops, and it broke him. The seed of hate had been planted deeply into his heart.

It didn't help that his life source – my mother – was not reachable. Mail came sparsely. On the rare occasions he did receive mail, he had a difficult time opening the letters for fear my mother would not want him anymore because of the atrocities he had done in the name of peace.

But he had nothing to fear, as my mother loved my father to no end. I was touched by her compassion for the man she loved. My mother never complained about his absence; she only talked about how wonderful it would be when he came home. She talked about her pregnancy with my sister and was excited when she spoke of the fine life together as a family when my father came home for good. She gave him hope.

My dad was careful in his responses to her. He didn't want her to know what his life was now like. He didn't want her ever to think he was the monster the war was turning him into. He kept their wedding picture next to his heart; she was his sliver of hope, and for that, he made it through every minute, every hour of the never-ending nightmare in Vietnam.

My sister was born two days before my father's first tour ended. He was on his way home and didn't learn he was a father until his father-in-law picked him up from the airport. My father broke down at the thought that he wasn't there to see his daughter being born. He went directly to the hospital to my mother and held her, held my sister, never leaving their sides the entire time they were in the hospital. My father promised my mother he would do whatever it took to get out of the military and be there for her and my sister. He promised never to leave them again.

But that promise was soon to be broken. My father tried in vain to stay stateside, but his requests fell on deaf ears. Soon after his leave, he was sent back to war. The Tet offensive of 1968 was legendary. And he had heard the horror stories, and they weren't pretty. My father had been back in Vietnam for nine months and had dreaded Tet the whole time. It was the end of January 1969 and Tet was upon him. My father was becoming numb, and the look of terror that had been in his eyes was turning into something else, almost dead. It was around this time he totally changed. Between the ongoing horrors and the harshness of his commanding officer, my father became completely broken. The man he used to be was gone.

I Died Yesterday

When my father came home after his second tour, he was nearly unrecognizable, not in appearance, but in spirit. The once happy, loving husband and father had become a sullen, bitter, and angry man.

I saw my mother as she struggled to do her best to lighten my father's life. She planned parties, dinners, and quiet time for them to bond as a family. My father was resistant to her attempts, but for the alone time. It was then he would let his defenses down and hold my mother, apologizing over and over again for not being the husband she deserved, the father my sister deserved. My mother comforted him, assured him everything would be all right. My father tried his hardest to push the horrors of war from his mind and be the man he knew his wife deserved. But good things don't last forever. My father was called back to duty for his last tour.

When he arrived in Cambodia on August 18, 1969, my father was assigned to the Second Brigade, 4th Infantry Division at A Khe, in the Central Highlands of II Corps. He spent most of his time screening for a division that was trying to avoid major battles before Nixon's troop reduction program. But as fate would have it, it wasn't to last.

More troops died around him. Trust was no longer a privilege he enjoyed. The enemy became every person around him. He hated himself for surviving as he witnessed his friends torn to bits by landmines, gunfire, and grenades. His commanding officer beat into his head that he was lucky, not smart. He told my father time and again that he should step up, fire more, and kill the enemy. Little did that commander know my father's worst enemy was himself. My dad became fearless, putting himself in the line of fire every chance he got and shooting at everything that moved. He killed children, women, anyone who came into his line of fire. He became a madman who broke to the point of becoming a determent to his squad. My father was dishonorably discharged from the military as mentally unstable. It was then my father came home. The hopeful, loving man who had planned a beautiful future with my mother had died in the killing fields. Only his shell came back.

Chapter Nineteen

It broke my heart to watch my father return to a country he no longer understood. There was outrage in the streets, unrest in the country over the war. There was no hero's welcoming; the war was not one looked at with pride, and it only made him feel more like a monster.

No longer interested in building a rosy future in his darkened world, my father decided going to school would be a waste of time and got a job working at the canning factory in town. He liked his job because he didn't have to think there. He worked in utter solitude, the only company the war that continued to play on in his head. Every night, he came home at five p.m., and if dinner was not on the table waiting for him, he flew into a rage. Even though my mother did her best to accommodate my father and to be understanding of what he had experienced, my father would direct his rage toward her, sometimes getting violent with her.

I was conceived in a rare moment of intimacy between my parents. My mother tried to make her pregnancy a happy event, but my father was not happy about another life entering his tortured world.

The day I was born, my mother had to call a taxi to get to the hospital because my father refused to leave work to bring her there. My mother's labor was extremely difficult, and she nearly died giving birth. My father was bitter about the fact that my very birth almost took the one person he loved away from him. It was heartbreaking to learn.

From my earliest memory, every night, sleep was disturbed by the screams and vulgarity that flew out of my father's mouth as he relived the war in his dreams. My father was tortured by his thoughts every waking moment, but the real trauma came out in his sleep. My mother would soothe him, calm him, and spent countless sleepless nights holding him, doing her best to comfort him. She had tried on a few occasions to learn more about what had happened to my father in the war, but he was silent, believing she would hate him if she really knew him. Over time, the silence of his thoughts took a toll on their marriage, and their relationship became distant, tolerant.

As I said before, my father was not a loving man or father. He was hard on all of us, because in his mind, he thought he was saving us from being the failure he had become. To show affection was to show weakness in his mind, so there was none in our home.

My father was an unpredictable tyrant. The slightest infraction of his rules, which changed constantly, provoked military-style punishment. Holding brooms over our heads as he whipped us was a favorite punishment of his. I spent my childhood in fear of the next punishment. Every day was like walking on eggs, never laughing in front of him, never speaking in front of him unless answering a question.

The damage my father caused ended the day he died of a self-inflicted gunshot wound to the head when I was eleven years old. His death was a relief to me at the time. As a child, I never understood why he was the way he was, but I know knew my father had finally become a casualty of the war he so deeply despised. I understood.

I had spent my entire life hating this man, never knowing that he once knew love. I felt an overwhelming sense of loss for that little boy who once had dreams of happiness and love. I felt sorry for not knowing how to reach my father. I was so disappointed in myself for never trying to reach the man who I knew was deep inside of him. For the first time, I felt love for him; love and forgiveness.

Chapter Twenty

The atmosphere in the house changed after my father's death. My father had been the sole breadwinner, as he had insisted my mother stay home to raise us and be a housewife. For the first time in her life, my mother had to go out and find work to support the family. With no skills, she went to work at the canning factory, taking over the vacant position created by my father's passing. She took some comfort in doing his job. She would say she felt closer to him every day she went in and did his work.

My mother worked grueling hours but did her best to try to balance home and work. Things were difficult for her and she found comfort in her evening cocktails. What started out as a glass of wine to unwind after a long day turned into a martini, then two.

When she drank, she would reminisce about my dad and the dreams they had together, dreams that never materialized. I would hear her crying at night when she thought we were asleep, and that broke my heart. I cursed my father for abandoning her, us, by being so selfish as to take his life. I of course had no idea why he had done so, which only made me more bitter at him for not giving my mother the life they had dreamed of.

My mother never spoke poorly of my father, and if we did, we were promptly punished for doing so. I loved my mother so much but couldn't understand her loyalty to a man who had abused her. Of course I understand now.

By the time I was nineteen years old, my mother was now drinking a bottle of vodka a day. She spiraled deeper into darkness and talked about how she wanted nothing more than to be with my father. I distanced myself from her because I didn't understand her and couldn't stand to watch her self-destruct.

My world, my life, came to a stop the day I found her lying in her bed, unresponsive, with an empty bottle lying next to her bed. I went to my mother and shook her in an attempt to wake her up. She was cold to the touch and then I knew she was gone. My mother had drunk herself to death in her struggle to live without my father. I lost the one person who loved me, who cared for me, who cared about me. I was devastated. Others tried to comfort me, telling me my mother was with my father and she was happy now. At the time, that was not the way I saw it. But now that my eyes had been opened, I hoped it to be true.

Chapter Twenty-One

Once again, I found myself in darkness, but this time, it was somehow different. I no longer felt the evil that had resided so strongly before. I felt as if I were floating on a waterless sea. It seemed I floated for what seemed like forever until I saw a shimmer next to me. All time seemed to stop as I heard a familiar voice, one I hadn't heard since I was ten years old. It sent a shiver through me.

"Terese?"

I looked toward the source of the voice and knew the voice I heard was that of my father. He was on his knees, his hands clasped before him, his face tired and lined. My heart went out to him.

My voice broke. "Dad?"

My father continued, "I have been waiting for you for so long. I am so sorry I failed you."

"Dad, you suffered so much!" I replied with tears flowing down my nonexistent cheeks. "I am so sorry your life went the way it did."

My father looked down, away from me. "You were my guardian angel. You were who I saw in my room when I was young. I saw you when I was on the battlefield. You were always with me. I am so sorry I never recognized that. I am so sorry I wasn't there for you; that I barely acknowledged you, that I hurt you. I am so sorry I was such a horrible father. I was so lost in my own misery, Terese."

Tears streamed down his face and the agony he felt was palpable.

"Oh, Dad, I understand. And I am so sorry you suffered. You did the best you could. I know that now."

Pleading, he said, "Can you ever forgive me?"

I stepped toward my father and took him by the hands. "Please, stand up, Dad." He stood up but kept his head down in shame. "Dad, I saw you as a little boy. I saw you happy. I saw your life, and I understand. I wish your life would have been better. I am not angry with you anymore because, truly, I understand. And, Dad, I love you."

My father seemed surprised by my response, but I continued, "Dad, I forgive you. I truly do. But can you forgive me for hating you?"

My father looked at me for the first time. The relief in his face, in his eyes, shone through. "Oh, my child, I understood your anger. I know that anger was well deserved for the way I treated you. There is nothing for me to forgive. If not for the way I was, you wouldn't have had those feelings. I am so sorry, Terese."

My father stepped toward me and wrapped his arms around me. He hugged me with so much warmth, so much love, I felt weak with emotion. All of the love I had missed out on in my lifetime from my father was replaced tenfold by the embrace he so tenderly held me in. For the first time in my existence, I felt whole as he held me. And it felt amazingly right.

After we had embraced and my heart could fill no fuller, we released one another. As I looked at my father, I saw him change. My father was no longer the man I knew. Before my eyes, he became the handsome young teenager I saw at that kitchen table many years ago. It was elating to see such joy in his eyes that was just indescribable.

It was then I heard the voice of a little girl. I looked down and saw a beautiful child, about three years old, standing next to my father, tugging at his hand, her face beaming as she looked up at him.

My father smiled a broad smile, reached down to the little girl, and took her hand. With delight, he said, "Terese, I would like you to meet your aunt, my sister Margie!"

"I know! Oh, Dad, I have missed you! I am so happy for you!" The pure joy in his eyes overwhelmed me, so much so, I was certain my heart would burst with happiness. His little sister saw my expression and broke into a huge smile as she danced next to him and giggled. I was overjoyed to see my father was once again with his beloved little sister.

"It's nice to meet you, Terese. Will you play with me sometime?"

"I would love that, my sweet Aunt Margie!"

At that, Margie looked back to my father as she pulled his arm and said, "Let's go, Tommy! It's time to go play!"

With that, my father turned to me, winked, and said, "I will see you again soon, Terese. You were my angel when I needed one most, and I will always cherish that. Thank you for forgiving me. I love you!" Then my father looked down to his baby sister and said, "Let's go now. It's time to play!" Margie squealed in delight.

My father reached into his back pocket, pulled out his baseball cap, and put it on his head. They turned from me and walked off hand in hand, giggling in glee and swinging arms as they faded from my vision.

Chapter Twenty-Two

Once again, I was alone, but this time, filled with conflict. I was happy my father had finally found peace and happiness in his life. It was so wonderful to hear my father, to see him, and to feel his love.

Though I had those feelings and was comforted by what I had just experienced, I found myself terribly ashamed for the life I had lived. Here I had spent my life judging others, not trusting those closest to me, and had been filled with resentment and hate when I could have opened my heart and found love.

Reflecting on my life made me fearful. I'd spent my life judging, and I was now nearing the moment of my personal judgment. What was going to happen to me for who I was and for what I had done? Who was going to forgive me when I knew I couldn't forgive myself?

Just the thought of how I had failed sent me into a despair that forced me deeper and deeper into the darkness. It seemed the depths of despair lasted for what could have been days, maybe even weeks – it felt as if it would never end.

I knew I didn't deserve forgiveness for what I had done to everyone in my life who tried to be close to me. I knew I hadn't been there for those who needed me. But, I told myself, how would I have known? No one said to me nor taught me, for that matter, how to love or how to care. It wasn't my fault, was it? Was it?

I knew my selfishness was not forgivable and the guilt of my actions was smothering. I cried out into the darkness, "Who will forgive me? I have not been a real person. I am a failed person, filled with hate. Oh God, who will forgive me now?"

I waited in a deafening silence, never expecting to get a response. Once again, I was wrong, because an answer did indeed come.

Chapter Twenty-Three

Suddenly, the atmosphere changed around me. It was if a switch had been flipped, turning the darkness into dawn. The change enveloped me, sending comfortable warmth throughout my very being in a way I had never experienced before. I felt as if I were being cradled in the bosom of motherly love and had been wrapped in a blanket made of soft summer clouds.

A rich, beautiful voice then spoke to me from nowhere and everywhere all at once. "My child, you are forgiven. I forgive you."

I knew instinctively whose voice I both felt and heard as it touched me to the depths of my soul. His voice humbled me. I threw myself onto my bodiless stomach; my face turned from Him in shame, not worthy of His presence. It was the voice of God.

"But how can you forgive me? My dear God! I have been so horrid to everyone around me my entire life. How can you forgive that?" I asked as I looked away from Him in shame.

God replied in a loving tone, "My child, I have always forgiven you. I love you. I have always loved you, so much, in fact, that I created you."

"Oh dear God, how could you forgive such a despicable person like me? I spent the life you gave me filled with hate, jealousy, judgment, and envy."

"Are you feeling those things in your heart now, my child?" God inquired.

I choked back tears in my response. "Oh no. I have seen what I did. I understand I was wrong in my all of my actions. I realized I needed to forgive those who I had judged so harshly. No, my dear Lord, I no longer have hate in my heart. For the first time in my existence, I finally feel love."

"But you don't feel complete love, do you?" God asked.

Confused, I replied, "What do you mean? I have never felt this much love."

With what sounded like a parent speaking to a wayward child, God spoke to me in a commanding voice. "There is more to love than you now know. You, my child, have the ability to a *become* love. But what happens next is up to you."

I pulled myself up to my feet and stood to cower before the Almighty. I asked with great humility, "What do you mean it's up to me? I don't understand."

God responded, "You have one person left to forgive, a vital person; someone who you have always considered to be of no value, to be unlovable and insignificant. Once you forgive that person, you will be free not just to feel love, but to be love."

My mind raced as I tried to comprehend what God was asking me to do and who else I needed to forgive to become something as spectacular as love.

Was it the woman at the cleaners who I treated so rudely because I thought she was taking advantage of me? Or could it be any one of my co-workers who I so openly despised because I was sure they didn't like me? Or maybe it was the bus driver who I ignored because of the way he looked at me? I was overwhelmed and sickened of myself as more and more images of experiences and people came to mind.

My self-hatred only grew as my life played out before me. There were countless people who I had judged, mocked, or even despised, all for no real reason. Oh, my dear God, there had been so many I had thought so little of, who I had treated poorly, all because of my closed mind and heart. How in the universe could there only be just one person left when I had left so many in my wake?

I threw myself down on my knees before Him and pled, "Who do I need to forgive, dear God? Please, I beg of you, who? There are too many people I have judged. Too many I never gave a chance. Please, dear God, my Creator, please tell me. Who?"

God spoke just three words in his loving, commanding voice. "You, my child."

I felt his presence leave just as quickly as it had arrived. Once again, I was alone with the most despicable person I had ever known. Myself.

Chapter Twenty-Four

God asked me to forgive myself, but how could I ever possibly do so? I had been a horrible human being, having chosen to refuse or give love, to forgive, or to even care enough to try to understand those around me. God was asking too much of me for me even to begin to forgive myself.

My soul seemingly rolled into a ball as I put my arms around my bodiless legs. For hours, days, weeks – I don't know – I rocked back and forth in the darkness, thinking of all the wrongs I couldn't right from my previous life.

My pity of myself grew until it was nearly out of control. The darkness around me gathered closer, becoming almost suffocating.

I finally reached the point where I was emotionally spent. I was numb; I had no more room in my soul for any feeling. I was worn out from beating myself up over things I couldn't change, for words I couldn't take back, for judgments I shouldn't have made.

It then dawned on me what God was asking of me. I had to accept my actions. I had to let the past go. I knew the anger I felt toward myself for the things I did had already been forgiven by the almighty God Himself and if God could forgive me, maybe I could as well.

It was not easy, but I found it in myself to remember me as that little girl who didn't know any better, the teenager who was lost and insecure after her father died, and the woman I had become who had built a wall to keep people and love out.

I forgave each of them, all of me, one at a time until there was nothing more to forgive. As I did so, I gradually felt warmth in my soul that I didn't know possible.

I thought of all those who had loved me, who had struggled through life, who did the best they could with what they had and I felt love for them as never before. I felt warmer still.

I realized I was only human and acknowledged the fact that I did not know how to react differently. I was imperfect, but that was okay. I knew I was no longer alone, as we are all imperfect. I was amazed to understand, that as imperfect as we are, God loves us, loves me, regardless.

Like a warrior at the end of the battle, I put down my weapons of hate, judgment, and disgust and waved the white flag of peace in my soul, surrendering the pain of the life I had lived. With that, I finally felt the forgiveness God had asked of me.

Chapter Twenty-Five

The air is now becoming lighter around me as I hear a sound as beautiful as the morning sunrise, as the angels sing their songs of love and adoration to our Creator.

It is magical, simply breathtaking, a chorus of angels that any earthly being would never be able to understand until they hear it themselves.

At this very moment, I am feeling myself being effortlessly lifted up, and to my amazement and absolute glory, I see a brilliantly stunning light, radiating warmth so heavenly I want to wrap myself in it and never escape.

It isn't a solid bright light; no, there are trillions of individual small lights, made of the souls who had passed before me, joined as one. Each light radiates love from their very essence.

A pure divine love, which is truly indescribable. When you feel this kind of love like I am right now, you will know true ecstasy. Knowing I am a part of that love is pure joy. I am finally free, I am with God, I am love, and I look forward to the time I can share that love with you.

My story is over now, as I am about to step into the glorious light, thrilled beyond imagination and bliss to join all those souls who have passed before me and to become one with God. You will see me there.

It is now finally time for me to say goodbye and to thank you for letting me share my story. I hope it has brought you some semblance of comfort. As I join my loved ones, your loved ones, I ask you to remember you are never alone. Through time and infinity, there is hope. There is Love. There is always love. God's love.

Made in the
USA
Lexington, KY